ESCAPE

by

D.W. Lewis

The Caerwyn Chronicles
Book III

A note from the Author:

Escape is a part of the larger series, The Caerwyn Chronicles that follows a single family from one generation to the next. These are not the powerful elite, they are the common, ordinary people that experience what the turmoil history throws at them. These stories deal with a very different time in society, when slavery was accepted, women were not treated with as much respect as today, and punishment was inhumane. While I write about these incidents, I am not trying to shock my reader with descriptions of these acts. My goal is to bring out the strength of the people who managed to survive these situations, not to drag others through the trauma.

This book has depictions of sexual assault, torture and slavery. They are not graphic, but please take care while reading.

All characters in this book are fictional, any resemblance to anyone living or dead are coincidental.

Part I

Escape the Past
92 AD

Chapter 1
Taran

The warm wind moved the sand around Taran's feet. He adjusted the scarf on his head and pulled it around to cover his mouth the way he had seen the locals do it. This was his second time coming to the big stone city. He remembered the first time he came to Petra, walking down the long canyon floor, tall red rocks towering over him. The canyon opened to the tall columns carved into the rock. It was awe inspiring.

Taran had grown up in Brittania, the son of an innkeeper. His father had taught him how to manage money, he enjoyed calculating costs and earnings. The people he admired most were traders, people who travelled the world and moved goods. For him trading involved two things he liked, travel and money.

When he turned seventeen, Taran joined a party of traders and traveled to the Greek islands. He managed to make enough money during the first few years of working with others that he set out on his own. Now at twenty years old he was leading a small group of traders to pick up spices to take to Londinium. He brought his group into the city, and they settled their horses down near a trough of water.

Taran turned to his business partner, a Greek man named Pyrros. Pyrros was an older man with dark hair and a bushy beard. He had a thick nose and dark eyes.

"You said you had a friend here?" Taran asked.

"Yes," Pyrros responded, "he owns a caravansarais near here. It's a little bigger than your caupona I think." Pyrros liked to tease Taran about the small inn his family ran. The Caupona Caureni was small with only three cubiculae for guests. It was on a small Roman road that went from Londinium to the northern limits of Roman control, so they could manage well enough with three rooms.

"Let's see if we can get a comfortable bed for the night," Taran said.

"That would be good," Pyrros said, clapping Taran on the shoulder. They called the other two men in their caravan and walked through the throng of people through another canyon to where the valley opened and a vast city became visible. Close to one of the canyon walls was the caravansarais they were seeking. A low stone building with small columns around it. Pyrros said it reminded him of Greece; it reminded Taran of the Roman buildings in Londinium.

They passed through a small entryway, which was low enough that Taran had to duck to get through. He was taller than most men, but still shorter than his uncle Cador, whom he had met once in his travels to Caledonia. Taran had dark hair and eyes, like most of the locals here, but his skin was pale and his nose was straight, so he still stood out. He removed his scarf and let his curly hair fall down to the nape of his neck.

The proprietor of the caravansarais, was a friend of Pyrros and gave them rooms at a reasonable price. Taran paid him with Roman coins and got a big smile in return. They were becoming more common here, but most traders hoarded them. Coming from a nation that didn't have its own currency before the Romans came, he traded mostly in Roman coins. He kept some Greek and Nabatean coins for use with the local merchants.

The room he was led to had stone walls and a small opening near the roof for light. There was a small bed, not ornate but functional and a table with a stool. There was a small basin with water for washing the dust off. For Taran this was enough. He closed the door and removed his tunic to shake the dust off. He then washed himself with the water from the basin.

Feeling human again, Taran went to the courtyard where they had food laid out for them. The food in Petra was nothing like at home, even when the Romans visited. The Nabatean people had specific spices they liked to use. The Romans went for anything, the Britons almost no spices. He got some roast meat and bread and sat with Pyrros.

Pyrros was sitting with two local men. He introduced them to Taran, the first was Malik ibn Sahr, and the second was Zandeil ibn Nūr. Malik was a stately looking Nabatean with a long grey beard and distinctive hooked nose. Zandeil was younger with a short beard and a straight nose.

"These men have brought oils from Judea to trade," Pyrros said. "They have fine olive oil, the Romans will pay well, I think."

"Good," Taran said, "we need to find out what they want to trade for the oil" Taran had learned Greek and some Aramaic, but Pyrros was fluent as he had traded in these parts for years.

"I am looking for Roman sestertii," Malik said in Latin.

"You speak Latin," Taran said with surprise.

"There seem to be more Romans here every year," Malik said, "only a fool would not learn to barter in their tongue."

"You are obviously no fool," Taran said, "where are you from?" Malik smiled, in his culture business was the last thing you discussed. This young man obviously understood that.

"I'm a traveler," Malik said. "My family have travelled to wherever the water is sweetest for generations."

"Interesting," Taran said, "my people are bound to the land, each generation makes the land richer with their blood."

"But you are here in Raqmu," Malik said with a smile, "what his people have named
Petra."

"The rock," Pyrros said with a smile, "a fitting name for this place." Malik nodded.

"Of course," Malik said. "Your people bring the rocks to their cities, we bring our cities to the rock." Pyrros and Taran laughed at his joke.

"How do you attend to your family if you move so much?" Taran asked, he loved learning how other people lived.

"Or family comes with us," Malik explained, "we have tents that we can carry and move from place to place."

"I've seen it," Pyrros said, "they take their whole house with them when they travel. It's something."

"I would like to see that some day," Taran said.

Malik said, "come tomorrow. I like you. I will send my boy Hagaru, he is learning Latin. He will bring you to our tent. You will sit and eat with me, and we will make a trade." Malik stood and Zandeil followed suit. Taran and Pyrros stood as well as the Nabatean men left. Things moved at their own pace here; there would be no trading today.

Chapter 2
Taran

Taran was always shocked at how warm this area could be, he and Pyrros had walked out of the city and after a short distance he was already covered in sweat. He adjusted his grip on the rope he was holding to lead the horse, the rough rope scratching at the palm of his hand. The boy Hagaru was used to the heat and moved quickly across the desert sand.

The tent appeared almost as if by magic in front of them. It was so well-hidden Taran didn't see it until they were almost inside. Hagaru led them to a small roped off area that held some horses and goats.

"They sleep here," Hagaru pointed at the horses and the other animals. Taran and Pyrros led the horses to the area. There was a girl waiting to take the horses in. She was beautiful, Taran had noticed that most of the Nabatean women were. She had dark eyes and complexion, with a gently curving jawline. Her hair was completely covered by her blue scarf, but he was certain it was as black as the night sky. He smiled at her as he handed her the rope. She averted her eyes but smiled back.

They moved on to a small tent that stood next to the main one. All the tents seemed to be made from woven hair and held up by long wooden poles. Instead of digging deep holes for the poles, they used ropes anchored by rocks to hold them up. Taran could see how this was all very easy to pack and move.

Inside there were woven mats covering the floor with cushions set out for comfort. The entire tent smelled of spices that Taran could not recognize. Malik was standing there to welcome them, and he invited them to sit.

"Welcome," Malik said as they sat, "you must be thirsty." He turned and called out something in his own tongue. Two girls appeared; their faces covered with their scarves. They were carrying clay jars and brought them forward and poured three cups of water. These were presented to the men, who drank.

"The water is very sweet," Pyrros said politely.

"We have always liked the spring here close to Petra," Malik said, smiling, "it is too busy here, soon we will move on."

"We are fortunate to be here when you are," Taran said. A flap in the tent opened and three women came in carrying trays of food. Taran recognized the blue scarf of the woman that helped with the horses. She placed a tray in front of him; this time she looked him in the eyes. It was definitely the same girl as before.

Taran looked at the trays, there was flat bread and dates. There was also a small bowl of what looked like milk. He looked to his host, waiting until Malik started before taking some of the bread and eating. Malik was drinking from his small bowl, so Taran picked up his. It smelled like milk, so he took a sip. The milk was rich and creamy, it had a stronger flavor than cow's milk, but not as strong as goat milk. He looked at it wondering what it was.

"From the camel," Malik said, watching his reaction.

"It is good," Taran said, "thank you." He wasn't sure if it was considered an honor to be given camels milk or just standard hospitality. Out of the corner of his eye, he saw the girl with the blue scarf staring at him. The girl next to her leaned over and whispered something and she nodded discreetly. The other girl now looked at him. He could tell by the sparkle in her eyes she was smiling.

The food was done and Malik called the girls over. He handed his tray up to one,

so Taran did the same. The girl with the blue
scarf took his tray, as she did, their hands
touched briefly. Her hand was warm and soft.

The soft touch reminded him of
Canna, the girl he could have married. They
were betrothed at a young age; he was sixteen
and she was thirteen. He could still picture her
light brown hair and fair skin; she had a very
angular jaw that he found beautiful. They had
held hands a few times during feasts and
festivals, which is what he remembered most
about her. Soft, warm hands.

When he had gone on his first journey
he had planned to bring back enough money
to set up a shop in his home village of
Caerwyn and marry her. When he got home,
however, he was told that she had died
suddenly. There was no warning, she fell ill
one evening and the next day she was gone.
Taran had mourned at home and realized that
the best way to move on was to do what he
really loved. He decided not to marry and to
see the world.

This had upset his mother; she wanted
to see him happy with children of his own. He
explained to her that he would be happy,
seeing everything the world has to offer.
Maybe one day he would marry, but it would
have to be a girl that understood the need to
wander.

Taran realized he wasn't paying attention to the negotiations that had started. Pyrros was looking at him. Pyrros chuckled.

"He's a young man," Pyrros said, "perhaps your daughters distracted him." Malik laughed at Taran's embarrassment.

"I was thinking of home," Taran said, "your hospitality reminded me of my father."

"A great innkeeper, the greatest in Brittania," Pyrros said, "you have been given great compliment!" Malik nodded his head discreetly.

"I should like to visit someday," Malik said.

"You are welcome," Taran said. He knew that Malik would likely never leave the desert, but Nabatean culture expected an invitation.

"Malik was saying that he has fifteen amphorae of oil from Judea," Pyrros said. Taran did some fast calculations in his head. When he was last in Londinium, Judean oil was selling for twenty sestertii per amphora. He would need a low price from Malik because he would need to get some camels for the trip to the port in Gaza.

"That will be well received in Londinium," Taran said, "we will need to get it to Gaza. That will add to our cost."

"Yes," Malik said, "it was costly to get here from Judea. Dangerous too with the uprisings there." Taran loved this part of the barter, each person explaining why they needed a better price for themselves.

"He's not wrong," Pyrros said.

"I'll need at least fifteen denarii per amphora," Malik said, spreading his arms out. Everyone in the room knew this was too high, but it was all part of the game.

"Once we cross the sea, we will end up having to use the oil ourselves at those costs," Taran said. Pyrros nodded along, he had taught the boy how to barter. When he realized that Taran had a head for numbers, he liked to sit back and watch him work.

"I see," Malik said, "the cost of business. I think thirteen is fair." Taran shook his head, but he knew they were close.

"Only if you deliver it to Gaza for us," Taran said as a joke. The cost of transportation was lower if they only needed to transport it from Gaza, but nobody would agree to deliver it there.

"Done!" Malik said, slapping his knee. Pyrros and Taran exchanged a look. What did he mean by that?

"You will deliver it to Gaza?" Taran asked.

"If I have a guarantee of thirteen denarii," Malik said with a smile. "We can go together. I will provide the camels, and you can pay for protection." Taran understood a little more now. The trail from Petra to Gaza was filled with thieves. There were no Roman patrols until you got close to Gaza, so thieves worked with relative impunity. The other two traveling with him were men he had hired for security in Gaul.

"We have an agreement then," Pyrros said. The men all stood and shook hands. Malik escorted them to where the horses were waiting. Somehow the same girl was waiting with the horses. Either Taran had been mistaken in the tent, or this girl moved quickly. She handed the ropes to the men and Malik seemed to give her a stern look.

"My daughter, Samira," Malik said pointing to the girl. Taran smiled in greeting, afraid if he was too forward, he would cause issues. They walked back towards the caravansarais, Taran silently repeating the name. Samira.

Chapter 3
Cador

The archway to the Caupona Cauperni stood firm, the sign with the triskelion hanging above it welcoming Cador home. He had received word that his brother Aedan had died and travelled back to Caerwyn to visit with his sister, Seren. As he walked through the arch he spent a moment thinking about the fact that he had never brought Lirra here. He thought he would have more time with her, but she had died young.

The courtyard had not changed, to the right were four doors, three guest cubicula and the bathhouse. To the left was the big kitchen with a brick oven and tables. A staircase led to a second level where he had lived as a child. Straight ahead was the entrance to the stable, where Cador had spent countless hours taking care of the animals. The courtyard also had a well in the middle making watering the animals and cleaning the inn easier.

A girl of fifteen or sixteen was in the kitchen, cleaning up. She had red hair and fair skin. Her ears were just a little bigger than you would expect and her chin had some harsh angles. She was clearly Aedan and Maeli's child. She saw him and walked over with a welcoming smile.

"Welcome," she said kindly, "are you needing a room for the night?" Cador smiled, she was Aedan's daughter.

"I'm looking for Maeli," Cador said, "she's the wife of my brother." The girls face lit up.

"That makes you Cador," the girl said. "I'm Maired. I'm Maeli's daughter! I'll get her." Maired rushed off to the kitchen. There was a small room off the side, divided by a curtain. It was the tabiculum, where the money was counted and kept. It had been his brother's favorite room. Maeli came out, she was still slender and carried herself with pride. Her hair was no longer red, but completely white. She still had a stern look though.

"Cador," Maeli said, "it's nice to see you again. Maired, go tell Seren her brother is here." Maired nodded and rushed out the archway to the road. Maeli invited Cador to sit in the kitchen while she poured two tankards of ale.

"Where is Seren?" Cador asked. He had not been here since he had gone to find his family. That had been twenty years ago, Cador was shocked at how quickly time passed.

"Her husband Owain has land not far from here," Maeli explained, "they raise cows and provide cheese and butter for most of Caerwyn."

"I think I remember Owain," Cador said. He took a drink of ale. It tasted like home.

"Still providing the same ale," Cador said with a laugh. They bought it from a local man; a friend of his father.

"We get compliments on our ale," Maeli said with a smile.

"I heard about Aedan," Cador said, "I'm sorry I didn't come home sooner."

"He would have been happy if you had," Maeli said, "but he knew travel between here and Caledonia is difficult." Cador nodded. The Roman guard at the frontier stopped a lot of people from coming in, suspecting troublemakers. Cador's size always caused them to suspect him. They sat quietly for a moment, each unsure of what to say.

Cador looked around again at the inn. He had many happy memories of being here. He and his brother used to practice with wooden swords in the courtyard. His father taught them a few things about fighting. Their sister would sometimes join in and then yell at them for playing too rough.

When his sister Seren came through the archway, both Cador and Maeli were happy to see her. Cador got up to greet her in the courtyard. Somehow, she didn't seem to have aged at all. Her blonde hair still shone in the light and her wrinkles all seemed to come from laughter.

"Cador!" Seren said, "you're here!"

"I am," Cador said, "how are you?"

"I'm doing well," Seren said, leading Cador back to the kitchen to sit with Maeli. "Owain and I live not far from here. We have two children, Llyr, he's eighteen now, and Teleri, she's fourteen. She's walking here now with Maired. I admit I rushed ahead."

"I'm glad things are going well here," Cador said. He thought he saw an exchange of looks between the women but didn't know what it meant.

"What about you?" Maeli asked quickly.

"My Lirra died a few years ago," Cador said, "we have Cyn, Lirra found him in a burned-out village, and we took him in. Riva is married now. She has her own son, Artor." Cador paused for a minute, then added "I've met your son Taran! He was coming through with some traders."

"He is still out trading," Maeli said sadly, "he doesn't know about Aedan yet."

"You're living alone now?" Seren asked.

"I have Riona," Cador said, "our slave, she's been with us for a very long time. We share a yard with Riva and Eiran, her husband."

They were interrupted as Maired returned with her cousin and walked up to the kitchen; they were giggling as they came in. Cador stood to greet them.

"I told you he was tall," Maired said to Teleri.

"As was my father," Cador said without thinking. That was his standard response to people talking about his height. Seren laughed at the comment. Their father had been very tall, it was comical to see her parents kiss, he would bend over in half to reach her.

Teleri was a beauty at only fourteen. She had a small nose that crinkled when she laughed and bright blue eyes. Her hair was straight and the color of brass. She giggled as she looked up at Cador.

"Good day," Teleri said, putting out a hand. Cador shook her hand and she smiled, her whole face lighting up.

"How about you two preparing some food for Cador," Maeli said. The two girls obediently went into the kitchen to organize the food.

"You will have men calling every day with those two," Cador said.

"Owain is very anxious to find someone for Teleri," Seren said, "once she is betrothed the boys should stop coming." Cador laughed. He remembered when Riva was that age, he had to choose the right man for her. There were many volunteers.

"Now," Maeli said, "you must want to get cleaned up and rest for a bit. You have your choice of cubicula; we have no guests. And the bath is available."

"I don't want to take a room that can be used for guests," Cador said. "I can sleep in the stable, I would enjoy a bath." It had been years since he had been able to use a bathhouse. Without another word he walked over to the bathhouse to get himself cleaned up.

Maeli and Seren sighed as he left. They didn't know how to tell him there had been very few guests after Aedan died.

.

Chapter 4
Taran

The tent was completely gone; there was no sign that it had been there at all. Taran was amazed at how efficient the Nabateans had been in packing up their home. Malik greeted them the camels were already loaded and ready to head out for Gaza.

They inspected the amphorae of oil, which had been sealed by a reputable Judean oil press. Pyrros was happy that everything was legitimate. He was also counting his profit on the endeavor. They had packed their horses with spices they had traded for in Petra. This had promise to be a successful trip.

As they were getting ready Malik brought two women and a young man over to meet them. The young man they knew as Hagaru and Taran recognized one woman as the daughter Samira. The older woman he did not recognize.

"This is my wife Layla," Malik said, "she will be in charge of the provisions. If you need anything, ask her. And you know Hagaru my son and my daughter Samira. They both speak some Latin and will be available to translate."

"Very good to meet all of you," Taran said. The trip would take between one to two weeks, so it was good to know who he could go to when he needed anything. Malik called out something in his native tongue and the caravan started on its way. Taran joined the men in front with the horses while the camels brought up the rear.

Malik had a few slaves to help drive the camels and had hired a few more men for protection. With the two hired men that Taran had they felt well protected against bandits. Taran often practiced with a sword in the evenings while traveling. He would ask anyone who could teach him how to fight. Growing

They had started when the sun was low on the horizon, but as it rose the sand quickly became hot and the air was suffocating. Taran focused on the horse in front of him, leading his own horse. The day quickly became tedious as they moved.

Taran let his mind wander, thinking of his various travels. He loved seeing new things and having new experiences. He had seen huge temples to the various gods in Greece and Rome. He wondered about those gods. Surely, they weren't all real.

His mother had taught him to read using a codex that had been given to her by a

man that had been enslaved with her years
before she married his father. It was written
by a man named Paulos about the Judean
God. Somehow, they managed with only one
God.

The sun was high overhead when
Malik called for a halt to the procession. They
had come up on a small spring. There was a
pool of water that was fairly small.

"This is where we must stop for the
day," Malik said, "it is too far to the next
oasis." He called out something in his native
tongue and the caravan stopped and the
encampment started to appear. Pyrros and
Taran watched with amusement as Malik and
his wife walked around telling the men where
to put various things.

Finally, Malik came back and called
Taran and Pyrros to bring their men to a small
tent. They realized it was the same one Malik
had used to greet them. He told them this
would be their tent. He informed them that it
was not allowed for them to enter any other
tent without permission from him. They
understood and agreed.

The tent was laid out the same as
before with cushions and woven mats. It was
dark in the tent compared with the outside,
Malik showed them how to lift one wall of the
tent and use poles to open things up and let

light in. Taran took his two men and went back to their horses. They unloaded the packs from the horses and led them to the pool of water.

After the horses drank, they went to the area that had been roped off for the animals. Samira was there directing the care of the goats.

"Do we have feed for the horses?" Taran asked her. She looked at him for a minute, obviously trying to understand the question and find the words to answer.

"We have, yes." Samira responded. "Leave here, I take care." She called over one of the men and directed him to take over with the horses.

"Thank you," Taran said. Samira smiled and turned back to what she was doing. Taran watched her for a moment. She was very confident in telling the men what to do and making sure all the animals had food. He shook his head as he walked off, that was the kind of woman he admired. Good at traveling and full of confidence needed to take control of things.

Taran went back to the tent to find that food had been delivered for them as well. Spring water, some meat and bread. He joined the men who were eating their fill. It was cool in the tent and quite comfortable. Malik came by to let them know that the caravan would leave before the sun came up in order to make it to the next source of water.

Taran settled in to enjoy the rest. Pyrros and the others decided to take a nap. After a few minutes listening to them snoring, Taran decided to get some air. He walked along the edge of the camp to the spring. Malik's wife, Layla was filling up some jugs with water. She saw him and stood.

"All is good?" she asked.

"Yes," Taran said, "just getting some air." Layla stood for a moment staring at him. He realized she didn't speak much Latin.

"Sorry, no understanding," Layla said, "I go get Hagaru." Taran put a hand up.

"No," he said quickly, "no need." He smiled to show there really was no need to talk. She smiled in return.

"You know the Greek tongue," she asked in Greek.

"Yes," Taran said.

"I know some Greek," she said with a smile. Taran would use Greek with her in the future. Layla started to bend down again when she noticed something behind Taran and her eyes got big. Taran turned quickly and saw a cloud of dust on the horizon. It was a sandstorm.

A sudden wind had picked up all the loose sand from the desert floor and was blowing everywhere. This was very dangerous for anyone in its path. Fortunately, they had already made camp so they could safely sit out the storm. Layla shouted something Taran didn't understand.

"The animals!" Layla shouted in Greek. Taran then understood. He rushed over to where the animals were, Layla close behind. Samira was already there getting the camels into a line and then having them lay down, facing away from the storm. She saw Taran coming and pointed to his horses.

"Bring horses here," she shouted. Taran grabbed the horses lead ropes and brought them to the far side of the line of horses. Samira brought him some rough wool cloth and showed him how to tie them around the horse's head to protect its eyes from the wind. With the horses facing away from the wind and these coverings they should survive. Provided they didn't panic.

Samira was now lining up the goats with the camels so they would be sheltered from the wind by the camel's bodies. Taran joined her to help. Layla joined in the effort. They finished just as the sand started to blow around them. Taran and Samira covered their faces with their scarves and got down close to one of the camels.

Samira gasped and called out. Layla was being pelted by the sand, she was not able to get to shelter. Taran stepped out and moved towards her. The sand immediately pelted him, tearing at his clothes and hurting his hands. He got to Layla and put an arm around her. He realized that Samira had joined him. She pointed off to their right. The three of them moved off to the right. It took all of their strength to move.

Taran quickly understood why Samira had pointed, there was a rope nearby. They could close their eyes and use the rope to guide them to shelter. The three of them moved as quickly as they could, using the rope as a guide. Finally, the rope came to a pole, Layla was in the lead and felt around until she found the tent that was supported by this pole. She opened the flap a little and fell through. Taran made sure Samira was through before going through himself.

He opened his eyes and found himself inside the big tent. The floor was covered with the same mats and cushions as their tent. There were dividers made of the same material as the tent. As Taran looked around Samira started to laugh. Then Layla joined her. The wind and sand continued pelting at the walls of the tent and they were safe.

"Thank you," Layla finally said to Taran. She put a hand on his arm; her hand was red and inflamed from the sand. He looked down at his hands and they looked the same. Samira came over and offered him a drink of water. He drank, feeling the cool water run over his throat. He didn't realize how raw his throat was until now.

"Come," Samira said, "we must join father." She led him to one of the interior dividers of the tent and went through. The Nabatean men were all in this section. Malik stood when he saw Taran.

"How did you come to be here?" Malik asked sternly. Layla answered him in her own tongue, and he immediately calmed and sat down, beckoning Taran to join him. "My wife says you helped her, thank you."

"She helped me," Taran said, "we worked together."

"Come, sit," Malik said, "we will need to wait for the winds to stop." The men sat down and the women went back to their part of the tent. Taran was very tired and closed his eyes for a moment.

When he opened them, he realized he had fallen into a deep sleep. Now everyone in the tent was asleep. He could tell that the winds had died down and wondered how the horses were doing. They might still be tethered and unable to move.

Taran quietly got up and snuck out of the tent so he didn't wake anyone. The moon was full and gave enough light for him to see without a lantern. He could see the animals were still tethered and went to free them. As he approached, he could see a figure moving around, checking the horses.

The horses were calm and seemingly unharmed. The person was removing the protective blankets and, using a lantern for light, checking the face of each horse. The lantern lit up her face and Taran realized it was Samira. She wasn't wearing her headscarf, and he could see her straight black hair glistening in the moonlight. She was beautiful in this light. He cleared his throat so she would know he was coming; she startled and quickly pulled her scarf up to cover her hair.

"How are they?" Taran asked.

"They are good," Samira said in her careful Latin. "No hurt." Taran nodded as he started to help untie the horses. He trusted her opinion since she had more experience than he did with sandstorms. He looked over at the camels who were sleeping like nothing had happened.

"How are your camels?" Taran asked, pointing at the beasts.

"They are strong," Samira responded. "They are made for sand." Taran had not spent much time with camels but had heard they were better suited for the desert than other animals. Samira called him over to one of the beasts.

"See?" Samira was pointing at the camel's nose. She showed him how the nose was capable of opening and closing. "No sand inside," she said. Taran shook his head in amazement.

"They are amazing," Taran said.

"Amazing?" Samira asked slowly. Taran realized she didn't know this word; he tried to think of another word she might know.

"It is," he thought and then widened his eyes and took in a breath as if amazed. Samira laughed and nodded.

"They are amazing," she said slowly. Trying to commit the word to memory. They went back to checking and untying the horses. One of the horses had some scratches on her lips and gums from the blowing sand. Samira got some water for the horse.

"It will heal," she said confidently. "Thank you for help," Samira looked into Taran's eyes. Her eyes were so dark, so beautiful. He felt like he could just lean forward and kiss her, but that would not be appropriate. He pulled himself away from her stare.

"I'm going to get more rest," Taran said, pointing to his tent. "We leave early."

"Yes," Samira said. Taran tried to decide if she sounded disappointed, but it was hard to tell with just a word. Samira put a hand on his shoulder and thanked him again before turning back to her tent.

Taran went back to his tent and found a place to lay down. As he stared at the roof of the tent, he thought about Samira's beauty. She was also remarkably strong, she had helped keep him upright while walking through the storm. They had held each other up.

Chapter 5
Maired

There was always so much work to do at the caupona that Maired sometimes felt the need to disappear for an hour or so. She had found a small hole in the back corner of the stable when she was ten and found that she could get through it and into the forest. Now that she had grown bigger the hole was almost too small, she needed to work to get herself through.

She enjoyed being in the forest, it was quiet and nobody expected her to do anything. She ran away from the caupona, her face full of joy as she jumped over fallen logs and around saplings moving as fast as she could. The wind blew her hair behind her as she ran to a small clearing that she knew about deep in the woods.

The sun was warm and Maired was hot and tired from her run. She spread out her cloak on the tall grass and lay down looking up at the sky. The clouds floated by, wispy and bright. Maired liked to imagine she was a bird, free and flying high above the clouds. She kept an eye on the movement of the sun, she knew her mother would be upset if she disappeared for too long.

As she lay there basking in the sun, a long shadow suddenly appeared, blocking the sun. She sat up, looking around and saw a boy standing over her. She let out a little scream, and he put his hands up defensively.

"I didn't mean to scare you," the boy said, "I wanted to make sure you were ok." He was a little taller than Maired and had short cropped brown hair. He had a thin nose and thin lips. She realized that he was dressed in a Roman tunic and cloak but wore trousers like a Briton.

"I was just watching the clouds," Maired said. The boy looked up and laughed a little. Maired was a little annoyed that he found that funny. She stood up and put her cloak back on.

"I'm Marcus," the boy said with a smile.

"I'm Maired," Maired said.

"I live at Eboracum," Marcus continued. As she expected, Eboracum was the Roman fort, this boy was Roman.

"You a legionary?" Maired asked suspiciously. He wasn't dressed as one, but surely, they didn't always wear their armor. The boy laughed again.

"I'm too young," Marcus said, "I'm a calō, I work at the fort and help my father." His chest puffed a little as he added, "he's a

Centurion." Maired knew little about the
military ranks in the army but assumed this
was important.

"That's nice," Maired said non-
committedly.

"Where are you from?" Marcus asked.
Maired shook her head, this boy was talkative.
She wasn't used to that from men.

"I'm from here of course," Maired
said.

"This field?" Marcus said with a laugh.

"No," Maired said, "I live at the
Caupona Caureni."

"I've been to the bathhouse there!"
Marcus exclaimed. A lot of the military
stationed nearby came to use the bathhouse.
Her father had charged a small fee for the use
of the baths. "I never saw you there."

"I usually work in the kitchen,"
Maired said, hoping that would be enough for
this boy and he would leave.

"I was just heading over to the camp
on the hill." Marcus said. Maired knew the
camp he meant. There was a small camp set
up on a hillside to the north.

"You better go then," Maired said,
"that's a long walk." Marcus smiled as his eyes
moved down her body, he was obviously
admiring her figure. As she had gotten older,

she had seen a number of men looking at her that way, but with him it didn't feel improper.

"I wish I could stay longer," Marcus said, "get to know you better. Maybe I'll visit you sometime." With that he rushed off towards the woods across the clearing and disappeared among the trees. Maired had never met anyone as strange as this boy.

Maired rushed home herself, not wanting her mother to realize she was gone. She wiggled through the hole. As she came through, she saw her mother standing there. She had been caught!

As a punishment she was made to clean the bathhouse. The entryway was an open room with hooks for clothes. The tiled floor had the pattern of the triskelion that hung over the archway. This was easy to clean, wiping down the benches and mopping the floor with a rag. The next room was a little more work than she liked.

As the room where the people scraped off the dirt and oils with a small metal scoop, this room needed regular cleaning. Without slaves, this wasn't done as regularly as it should be. Maired understood why her mother didn't want slaves. As a freed slave herself, Maeli had sworn that she would never force another person to work for her.

Sometimes Maired wished there was someone else to give these tasks to.

The small tub in the hot room was emptied and Maired was made to scrub all the slime off the walls and floor. She finally got all that done and got their servant, Eòin to help her fill the tub again. They didn't empty the bigger pool as often and so she just cleaned it as well as she could, the task took all day, and she was not happy for one minute as she did it.

After she was finished her duties in the kitchen remained. She spent time in the cleaned bathhouse to get the grime off herself before rushing to the kitchen to work on making the evening meal. There were still no guests, so it was an easy meal to prepare. Maired had learned her lesson. She would need to find a new way to escape.

Chapter 6
Taran

After three days of walking from one watering hole to the next, Taran was getting bored. The landscape never really changed, low bushes, dead grass and sand. He had heard that if the rain hit the desert, it became a sea of green, but he had never seen it. During this time, he had not seen much of Malik or his family.

After the storm Malik had made a point of thanking Taran for returning to his own tent. He explained that privacy was important to his people. Taran explained that he understood, his family always kept their own space away from guests as well.

As they moved across the top of a hill, Taran could look out and see a great plane in front of them. It looked like a vast sea, but Taran knew it was a trick of the desert. There would be no sea, not even a drop of water. He was fortunate to be traveling with people that knew how to find water.

The air was stifling and Taran dropped his eyes to the trail in front of him. It was easier in the heat to move methodically, focusing on each step. He had a skin of water slung over his shoulder. He swung it up to take a drink, being careful not to spill when an arrow flew past his head and struck the ground.

"Bandits!" Taran yelled as he pulled the horse away from where the arrow had come. The others were moving quickly gathering around in a circle, the big camels on the outside. Taran drew his sword and moved between two camels to face the raiders.

Two of Malik's men appeared at either side of him carrying small bows and quivers of arrows. They searched the hills for a target. One obviously found one and let his arrow fly. He was rewarded with a cry of pain. Taran still couldn't see any of the bandits.

Another arrow flew but there was no sign it had hit anyone. Taran looked around at his group, they had taken positions around the circle, but most were just standing at the ready. He heard a cry from one of his men, arrows were coming from the hills. One of his men was hit. Taran could do nothing, but from the corner of his eyes he saw a flash of blue fabric moving to the fallen man. Someone was helping him.

An arrow flew by Taran again and he saw a man with a bow in the hills. He pointed and the man next to him shot another arrow. The man he had seen fell. Taran realized the bandits could sit all day and shoot down on them. He walked back a little way and found Malik.

"I'm going to take some men out to find them," Taran said firmly.

"Good," Malik said, then called out something in his own tongue. Hagaru and Samira led out a man Taran had never seen before. He was wearing Nabatean clothes, but his lighter complexion and lighter brown hair made Taran think he was Roman. He also carried a Roman sword, not the slightly curved blade of the desert. This was not the time to worry about who this man was.

Taran gathered Pyrros and his remaining man and they followed Hagaru and Samira into the desert. Getting down low, they moved swiftly across the desert floor away from the protective circle. Taran followed Samira, impressed with her ability to move quickly across the ground. They found a hollow in the ground and quickly gatherred to plan their next move.

Hagaru looked at the assembled group and took quick stock of the men. He looked around at the landscape and seemed to be taking note of where the arrows were coming from. He turned and looked at the group.

"You, and you" Hagaru pointed to Pyrros and their other man, "see the tree there. They are there." Pyrros nodded and tapped the other man's shoulder. The two men went quickly towards the tree. Hagaru turned to Samira and spoke in his native tongue. She tapped Taran's shoulder and Hagaru nodded.

"Come," Samira said softly. Taran followed, as he was crawling out of the hollow he heard Hagaru address the other man as Gaius, a Roman name. Taran shifted his focus swiftly to following Samira. They stayed low and moved behind an outcropping of rocks. Taran could see two bandits hiding.

Samira pointed at herself and then a bandit close to them and then to Taran and a different bandit. She meant for them to divide and conquer. Taran watched Samira walk slowly towards her target and then went quietly towards his own. They were almost upon the men when they were spotted, and the men yelled out, turning to fight.

The man Taran was fighting brandished his sword and yelled something at him. Taran stood firm and waited for the man to make his first move. The man swung the sword which Taran parried with ease. Taran realized the man did not know how to fight sword to sword. Taran lunged and caught the hem of the man's tunic with the tip of his sword, tearing it away.

The man got anxious and swung his sword wide, which was a mistake. Taran stepped into the swing and the man's arm bounced off his shoulder. Taran lunged again and this time his sword ran the man through. The man started gasping for air, Taran could smell the garlic on the man's breath they were so close. Taran pulled his sword back, which took all his strength and the man fell forward to the ground. Taran turned to see Samira standing waiting on him. She had apparently dispatched her opponent faster than he had.

"Mine was not used to using a sword," Taran said quickly.

"Mine was not thinking to fight a girl," Samira said with a laugh. "Come," she grabbed his wrist and pulled him along towards the hollow. He could see that Hagaru and the Roman were also on their way back. In the hollow they bent low to hide and Hagaru looked around at the landscape.

"Four more," he said, pointing off towards a clump of shrubs. Taran was not sure how he saw them, but after their previous encounter trusted him. The four of them went around behind the shrubs. There were four men with bows shooting down on the caravan. Hagaru and Samira nodded to each other, communicating without talking.

They leapt forward shouting an undulating cry that startled Taran.

Taran added his own battle cry, and heard the Roman add a yell. The four archers turned to face the new threat, grasping for swords. Hagaru killed one before he could find his sword. Samira met another sword. Taran did not see what the Roman did as he clashed with a third man.

This one was competent with a sword and parried his first thrust. Taran parried the man's return thrust and swung his sword slightly to the right to get the man to follow with his sword. When the man did, Taran stepped forward and used his body to push the man back. He lost his footing and stepped away from Taran. Taran stepped into the man again and saw a glint of steel as someone slashed at the man's head from behind.

Hagaru had already started back for the caravan, Taran and the Roman followed. The arrows had stopped; the bandits were either dead or escaped. As they came up, Pyrros was taking charge of the horses while Malik was organizing his men.

"Three dead," Malik said as they approached. "One is your man. It is too hard to bury him here, I think."

"What will you do with your dead?" Taran asked, "we will do the same."

"We will bury them in Gaza," Malik said. He pointed to where Lyla was directing men to wrap the dead up in cloth. "They will ride on a camel." Taran shook his head sadly; they died for no reason except to bring olive oil to Gaza. The Roman joined them and looked over at the dead bodies.

"The dust returns to earth," the Roman said, "the spirit to God." Taran looked at him quizzically. "From the sacred writings of the Hebrews, I spent many years living among them."

"So, you have met our other guest," Malik said, "he has asked us for safe passage to Gaza."

"I am Gaius," the Roman said, "I offended some of my fellow Romans by rejecting their gods." This made no sense to Taran; how did you reject gods? Gaius offered no other explanation than this, so Taran offered a hand and they shook. He introduced himself and the rest of his party. Those that were left.

Chapter 7
Maeli

With Cador gone the caupona seemed desperately empty. It had been nice to have him there, even if it was a practical stranger. He was Aedan's brother, which made him family. Maeli walked to the arch and looked out. There were people passing by, but nobody was stopping. She didn't know why, it didn't make any sense to her. Maeli sighed and went back to the kitchen. Eòin was getting himself some ale and offered to pour her one as well. She agreed and they sat down.

"I'm not sure we can keep paying you," Maeli told Eòin sadly. Aedan had decided long ago that the inn would run without keeping slaves. They had hired Eòin to help many years ago and he had become like family.

"I understand," Eòin said with a sad smile. "I enjoy working here. I have no real need for money, you continue giving me a room and food and I'll work for you." Eòin had never married and lived in the old slave quarters, Maeli couldn't guarantee food, but the room was there.

"Deal," Maeli said. As they shook, a group of Romans walked through the arch. A Roman officer and some of his men. Maeli still had a hard time talking to anyone from the legion but stood and approached them. She prayed to the gods they wanted to stay the night.

"Welcome," Maeli said hopefully, "welcome, do you need a room?"

"We are here for your bathhouse," the officer said sternly.

"Yes," Maeli said, trying to hide her disappointment. "We charge two asses per person." The officer nodded his head. "We will ask another three asses if you want an attendant." The officer shook his head, but counted out the coins, handing them to Maeli. She counted them and saw he had paid for the attendant.

Maired was walking across the courtyard when she saw the group. She stopped and stared at them for a moment and then turned to walk to the stable. Maeli noticed that a member of the group of men, a boy about Maired's age stood a little straighter when he saw her. She also noticed that Maired was swaying her hips a little more as she walked. Maired was starting to attract attention, Maeli needed to find someone for the girl to marry.

The men went to the bathhouse and Eòin rushed from the kitchen to join them. Maeli wondered if the fire would be hot enough for the bath. She walked to the stable where the small stove was located behind the bathhouse to heat up the water. Maired was already building up the fire.

Maired finished and walked past Maeli without comment. She hadn't talked much since Maeli had caught her sneaking out. Maeli felt sorry for the girl, she had lost her father, and her brother was out having adventures and she was stuck here. Maeli followed her to the kitchen and asked her to sit for a minute. She sat with as much attitude as she could.

"I want you to know," Maeli started, "I know why you are sneaking out."

"Do you?" Maired asked with a sneer? She would never have tried that with her father. Maeli sighed.

"I'm working you too hard," Maeli said, she saw Maired's guard drop a little. "I need to let you have some time to yourself, I'm sorry I haven't." Maired's face fell and she looked about ready to cry. Maeli put a hand out and Maired put her hand in her mother's hand.

"I miss Da," Maired said softly.

"Me too," Maeli said. They sat for a moment in silence together. A young man came out of the bathhouse draped in one of the togas they provided for modesty. Maired

was the first to see him and averted her eyes
as he came towards them. Maeli turned to the
young man.

"If I may, Domina," the young man
said. "We'd like some ale." Maeli still wasn't
used to being called Domina, that was the
term she was required to use as a slave.
Maired stood to start pouring the drinks.

"How many?" Maired asked, keeping
her eyes on the young man. She had
recognized him as he had come in, this was
the boy she had met in the clearing. She had
not noticed how muscular he was before. She
could see more of him in the toga and had to
admit she enjoyed what she saw.

"Five," the boy said. Maired tried to
remember his name, her mind went back to
their first meeting. She remembered he was
handsome, but also a little annoying. She
poured out five tankards of the ale and placed
them on a tray.

"I'll bring them," Maired suggested, to
Maeli's surprise. Maeli watched her daughter
follow the boy to the entrance to the
bathhouse. She had seen the boy's appearance
as well and was a little amused as she watched
Maired do something so out of character.
Usually, she had to insist that her daughter
help a guest.

Maired stayed close to the boy, trying to remember his name. Then she remembered. As they came to the middle of the courtyard, she caught up with him.

"Marcus," Maired said, "what are you doing here?"

"My father, the Centurion," Marcus stated proudly, "is in the village on business and wanted to clean up before the walk home. It was my idea to come use your bathhouse." He smiled at her as they approached the door, Marcus opened it and Eòin was waiting on the other side. He took the tray from Maired as Marcus walked by. As Maired handed the tray to Eòin she watched Marcus over Eòin's shoulder. He took his toga off as he walked through and Maired got a glimpse of his backside before she turned away. She just wished he was less talkative.

Maeli watched her daughter walk away from the bathhouse with a mischievous grin on her face. She would have to watch that girl! Aedan had been better at dealing with her, Maeli just didn't know what to do. Maeli recognized that Maired had the same determination that she had.

As the afternoon went on, the men in the bathhouse continued to order ale. Fortunately, now they sent Eòin out for it instead of the boy. Maeli noticed that Maired found tasks to do close to the courtyard so she could watch for the boy. Eòin finally came and announced that they would be coming out soon and would like some cold meats, cheese and bread before heading out. This was good news because Maeli could get more money from them.

The men returned looking refreshed from their bathing. The ladies had put together some pork, beef, mutton, cheese and some bread. Maired had learned to make some of the sauces the Romans liked, Maeli never liked the strong flavors and avoided them. It was a meal worth at least a sestertius. The soldiers ate hungrily and asked for more. Maeli provided the food and finally time came to settle up. The officer took Maeli aside to discuss the money.

"A sestertius for the food," Maeli said gently, hoping he would not try to barter.

"Of course," the Roman said, "a fair price." He placed the coin on the kitchen counter. Maeli smiled and left it there, not wanting to appear needy. "Your inn is quiet."

"We like it that way," Maeli lied, hoping the Roman would not guess the inn was in financial trouble.

"Me too!" said the officer. "My name is Quintin Tiberius, Centurion of the first century, second cohort, ninth legion, Hispania."

"I'm Maeli," Maeli responded..

"I need to be visiting this village on occasion for official duties," the Centurion continued. "I would like to set up some meetings here next time I come. Can that be arranged?"

"Of course," Maeli said, "we will make our caupona available for Rome." She felt a little strange saying that, but knew it was the kind of thing Aedan said to make Romans happy.

"I will send my boy, Marcus," Quintin pointed to the young man who was currently watching Maired sweeping the courtyard. "He will come the day before we arrive," Quintin continued, "we will pay for his accommodation for the night when we arrive."

"Very well," Maeli said, "we will watch for him." She didn't like the idea of the young boy being here, but it was the promise of having paying customers that made her agree. She would just have to watch her daughter around the handsome young Roman.

Chapter 8
Taran

As they set up camp next to the spring, Malik came to tell Taran that they should arrive in Gaza by the end of the day tomorrow. It had been a long trip, and one of his men was dead. Taran was glad to see the end in sight. He and Pyrros opened a jar of wine to celebrate the success of their journey so far. As they were drinking and feasting Gaius the Roman came to join them. He had spent some time with them during the last few days, enjoying speaking Latin with people that could understand it well.

"Men," Gaius said, "it has been an honor travelling with you."

"It has been good to travel with you as well," Taran said. "Come join us." Gaius sat to eat with the men.

"I am wondering where you are headed next," Gaius said.

"To Gaul, and then Briton," Pyrros said.

"Your home?" Gaius asked Taran.

"Yes," Taran replied. "It has been a long time."

"Do you have family there?" Gaius asked.

"My parents and my sister," Taran
said. He didn't like to think of them much.
While he enjoyed his travels, he missed them.
His sister had been a child when he left, she
would likely be a woman now, and betrothed.
He hoped her betrothal would work out
better than his.

"I am sure you miss them," Gaius
said, reading the expression on his face.

"I do," Taran said, "do you have
family?" Gaius looked down at the food in
front of him.

"I had a wife and daughter," Gaius
said, "they are with Iēsus now."

"Iēsus?" Taran asked. He had read
that name in the codex that his mother had
given him.

"I am a Christian," Gaius said, "a
follower of the teaching of Iēsus Christos."
Taran had never met someone that followed
the teaching before. This would be how he
had rejected the Roman gods, Taran had read
about the one God of the Christians, he tried
to remember the passage.

"Since God is one, he sets right those
he has set aside through faith," Taran said
softly. Gaius looked at him with surprise.

"Where did you read that?" Gaius
asked.

"A codex my mother gave me," Taran said, "a letter from a man named Paulos," Gaius shifted to his knees in excitement.

"Do you have it?" Gaius asked, "can I see it?"

"It is at the caupona," Taran said, "it is too valuable to bring with me." Gaius sat back, a little disappointed.

"I have read a few of the letters of Paulos," Gaius said, "he was an apostle of Iēsus Christos, a teacher of the way." Taran didn't know all of this. He had found the writings interesting, and the concept of a single God made him wonder. Was it possible for a single God to do everything that is required. Paulos also wrote about moral failure. How each person was guilty of not doing what was right. Taran had seen some things done that he disagreed with morally, and assumed he did things that others disagreed with. It made sense that all were guilty.

"This one was written for the people of Rome," Taran said.

"I've not read that one," Gaius said. He sat thinking for a moment and then asked, "would you mind if I joined you? Come visit your caupona?"

"You are welcome," Taran said, "I think my mother would like to meet you."

With that agreed the men made arrangements for Gaius to replace the man who was killed as part of the expedition.

After two weeks of travel with only a small group, Gaza was an assault to the senses. It was loud and dirty. There were people everywhere, traders, locals and Roman legionaries. Taran enjoyed Gaza, it still had the exotic feel of being in the east, but also some of the influence of the culture he was used to.

He and Pyrros went to the docks to talk to some shipping companies. It took all day, but they were able to secure passage in a ship that would be leaving in a week. This was good timing as they would need to sell their horses and make sure this leg of the journey was finalized. They found a small caupona on the edge of the city and settled in for the week.

Pyrros suggested that after eating they should take advantage of the bathhouse to scrape off the dust and sweat of travel. As they were in the tepidarium, scraping the dirt off their skin, they were surprised to see Malik come in to join them. They greeted each other kindly and Malik sat on one of the wooden benches. As they decided to move on to the caldarium, the room that held the hot water pool, Malik took Taran aside.

"I have business of a personal matter to discuss with you," Malik said softly. Taran nodded and the two found a bench in the caldarium and sat. This room was very warm and was filled with steam. Even though they had just travelled through the desert, the moist heat felt good.

"What can I do for you?" Taran asked.

"I have been very impressed with you," Malik said, "I would like to continue to trade with you." This was good news for Taran, any relationship with a Nabatean trader could be profitable.

"I would like to continue to trade with you," Taran said with a smile.

"Yes," Malik paused and looked out at the pool of water. He seemed unsure of what to say next. "My daughter is also impressed with you."

"I'm impressed with her," Taran said, "she is strong and resourceful." Malik nodded. Again, he seemed unsure what to say next.

"We Nabatean people," he started, "are a private people." Taran was wondering what he was trying to say. "Very rarely do we invite people from outside in. We have a strange problem." He paused and stared into the pool.

"If I can help," Taran said, "I would like to." Malik's face lit up and he turned to Taran.

"I'm glad you say that" Malik said, "I am looking for someone worthy of my daughter. I think I have found him." Taran still didn't know what Malik was talking about.

"Wonderful!" Taran said, "he will be fortunate." Malik laughed.

"He is you," Malik said as he laughed. "You are the one I would like my daughter to marry." Taran was shocked. He admired Samira and was truly impressed with her strength and resolve in hard times. Could he marry her?

"That is a good offer," Taran said, "can I think about it?"

"Of course," Malik said, "and if you do marry, it will have to be soon. Before we part ways, I think." While Taran understood that, it was still something to consider.

"I will have an answer by the morning," Taran promised. He wasn't sure he could answer by the next day, but it would have to be soon. The men stood and joined the others in the hot pool. Pyrros gave Taran a quizzical look, but Taran shook his head to say they would talk later.

Taran sat quietly and considered the options. If he married, he would have a wife that was used to travelling, she might insist on it. He would also have the advantage of her business sense. Nabatean women were known to be as skilled in trading as the men. He wondered what the people in Caerwyn would think of her. That was the only downside he could think of. He knew there would be some people in his home town that would not approve of her.

His mother would love her, so would his father. The last time he had seen his sister she was still a girl, she would be a woman now. He wondered if they would get along. The opinions of anyone else didn't matter. Taran was so lost in thought that Pyrros had to tap his arm when the time came to move on to the cold pool of water.

There really was only one remaining question for Taran as he followed the others to the cold pool. Did he want to be married? When he had been betrothed, he had taken it as fact that everyone got married. He had learned that wasn't always true, some people did not settle down and get married. He wondered if he wanted to settle down. With Samira he might not need to settle down. She was beautiful, he would have a hard time finding another woman as beautiful as she was.

They left the cold pool and dried off before dressing and heading out. Malik bid them farewell while Gaius went to his cubiculum. Pyrros followed Taran and asked what was on his mind.

"Malik has asked if I will marry Samira," Taran said.

"By the gods," Pyrros said, "what did you say?"

"I'm taking a day to give him my answer," Taran said.

"What are you thinking?" Pyrros asked.

"I'm thinking of saying yes." Taran said.

Chapter 9
Maired

Maired ran through the forest. The wind blew her hair back and her cloak fluttered behind her. Her mother had given her the morning off; she was free and didn't have to sneak around. When she got to the clearing, she laid her cloak down and lay down to stare up at the sky. There weren't as many clouds in the sky, but she still enjoyed staring up and daydreaming.

She imagined that she was with her brother, exploring the world. He had told her about Greece and the big temples, surrounded by columns and statues of their gods that were so tall they nearly touched the sky. She wondered what it would be like to travel on a boat. Her mother had been on a boat from Rome years ago and said it was terrible.

There were some birds in the woods nearby that were calling to each other. Maired wondered why they were saying to each other. It sounded like they were angry with each other. Taran once told her that birds tell each other that they own the tree. She laughed at the idea of one bird telling another to leave them alone. She laughed at the thought.

"What's so funny?" a male voice asked. Maired jumped up to find Marcus standing a short distance away. He had on a red cloak and a blue tunic. He was handsome. Maired was annoyed he was here.

"I was thinking about what the birds are saying," Maired said in an annoyed tone.

"I don't think they say anything," Marcus replied. "Just a lot of noise. Why do you like to lie in this field?"

"I just do," Maired really wished he would go away. Instead, he took off his cloak and lay down close to her. She sat there glaring at him, but he just looked up at the sky. She noticed he wasn't wearing trousers; it was warm today. He had muscular legs and he was wearing a white subligaculum under his tunic; she needed to stop nothing these things!

She lay back down and tried her best to ignore him. Thankfully he stopped talking, she was amazed he could. She could still feel him close to her. She could hear him breathing. Maired felt a little violated, her private spot was no longer hers. She wanted to leave and head home, but that felt like letting him win. Instead, she lay there and fumed. She realized he had propped himself up on an elbow and was looking at her.

"My father says you must be Caledonian," Marcus said suddenly. Maired didn't know how that was any of his concern.

"My mother is," Maired said.

"He said only Caledonians have hair like yours," Marcus continued. Maired sighed and kept her eyes on the sky. She could sense him coming closer. "Why isn't your mother's hair red?"

"It was," Maired said, "it turned white when I was a child."

"It's pretty," Marcus said, "you're pretty." Maired had never had a boy say she was pretty. She wasn't sure how to respond. She just stared up at the sky. Marcus lay down again but had shifted enough that he was right next to Maired.

"I should go," Maired said, about to stand. Marcus's hand caught hers and he held on to her.

"Wait," Marcus said. Maired was a little surprised at herself, she realized she wanted to stay. She moved her hand away from his but stayed.

"Why do you want me to stay?" Maired asked.

"I wanted to ask," Marcus stated, then stopped for a moment. Maired realized he was searching for the words to say, which amused her. "Are you betrothed?" Maired wasn't sure why he would ask this.

"No," Maired said.

"Oh," was all Marcus said. His hand was right next to hers, Maired could feel him moving it. He started rubbing her hand with his finger. She thought about moving it, but it also felt nice. She realized he had asked about betrothal because he was interested in her.

"Marcus," Maired said, "I think you are handsome too." He popped up onto his elbow and looked into her eyes. His brown eyes filled with longing. Maired laughed and moved so she looked past him. There was a bird flying overhead. She watched it as she wondered what she was doing. He was annoying sometimes, but he was also kind.

"I would like to kiss you," Marcus said. Maired turned her head to look into his eyes again.

"That might be fun," Maired said. She was surprised by her own words. She needed to get away; she jumped up, grabbed her cloak and rushed off. She ran towards the woods, laughing as she ran. She could hear Marcus running behind her. She stopped and turned to face him.

Marcus came up to her and stopped a short distance from her. He was smiling and he stepped slowly to get close to her. Maired

stood and let him get close. She was breathing
heavily and found that she was smiling too.
As he came closer, she leaned in and kissed
him. He wrapped an arm around her waist
and pulled her close.

Maired pulled away for a moment and
took Marcus by the hand. She led him back to
the middle of the field and lay down again,
pulling him down next to her. She lay on her
back, holding his hand. She stared up at the
sky again and giggled. Marcus turned so he
was facing her, he didn't let go of her hand.

"That was fun," Maired said. She
turned to face him; he was so close that she
kissed him again. As she kissed him, she
realized how inappropriate it was to be kissing
a boy lying in the field. She didn't care. They
continued kissing for a while, until finally
Maired realized how late it was. She jumped
up.

"What's wrong?" Marcus asked.

"I need to get home," Maired said.

"I need to get there too," Marcus said,
"we can walk together!" Maired wasn't totally
sure that was a good idea, but he took her
hand and she realized they could hold hands
until they got out of the forest. She liked the
idea of that. They walked together, heading to
the caupona.

"Why are you coming to the caupona?" Maired asked as they walked.

"My father is bringing some men up tomorrow," Marcus said, "I'm supposed to arrange some meetings with some of the local merchants."

"Are you spending the night?" Maired asked.

"Yes," Marcus said. He pulled her hand to his lips and kissed it. Maired wasn't sure she could handle having him so close, but would not be able to touch him. She realized how strange that thought was. This morning, she wouldn't have thought of him this way, now she found herself wanting his touch.

As they came to the back of the caupona, they let go of each other's hands reluctantly. Maired was relieved that the courtyard was empty, as was the kitchen. She took Marcus to the kitchen and sat him at the table. She poured him a tankard of ale and rushed up the stairs to find her mother. Maeli was sitting at a table in her room reading from a codex, several pieces of parchment sewn together. It was the only one they owned, given to her by an old man years before Maired was born.

"Ma," Maired said, "that boy from the Roman camp is here." Maeli stood and rushed down the stairs, Maired close behind.

"Welcome," Maeli said, greeting the young man.

"Domina," Marcus said politely, "I have come to make arrangements for the Centurion and several men to come here tomorrow."

"How many men?" Maeli asked.

"At least ten," Marcus said, "I will give you an answer this evening. I am to go now and invite them and see who will come." Maired was making herself look busy in the kitchen. She was impressed with how polite and official Marcus was.

"I will make arrangements," Maeli said. Marcus made a point of thanking Maired for the ale before heading out. Maired watched him leave, his broad shoulders making her long to be in his arms again.

The afternoon went so slowly, even though her mother kept her busy, Maired kept watching for Marcus to come back through the arch. He was taking so long. Maired thought about sneaking down to his cubiculum after her mother went to sleep. That would be wrong and she knew it, but it didn't stop her from thinking about it. Finally,

as the sun was setting Marcus came into the
courtyard. He looked exhausted.

Maeli prepared a meal for him, and he
sat by himself to eat. Maeli felt sorry for him
and suggested that, as he was a similar age to
Maired, she offer to sit with him. With a
warning not to talk too much, Maired rushed
to him before his mother could change her
mind.

"Mother said I should make sure you
aren't lonely," Maired said softly, "nod your
head, I'm supposed to be asking permission."
Marcus smiled and nodded.

"That would be nice," Marcus said.
"I've been thinking about this morning, I
enjoyed it." Maired quickly looked to make
sure her mother didn't hear. She was walking
to the stable, likely to make sure the fire was
going for the bathhouse.

"Me too," Maired said.

"Come my cubiculum tonight,"
Marcus said softly, putting his hands on hers.

"I shouldn't," Maired said with a
frown, she had been hoping he would ask.
Now that he had she was nervous. He looked
so forlorn, she grabbed his hand and said, "if
I can get away." He smiled back. Maeli came
back to the kitchen, so they released hands.

"Domina," Marcus said to Maeli,
"there will be five men coming from town,

my father is bringing three men and there is
me. The total will be nine men. My father will
want food and drinks. They will likely use the
bath after. I was told that my father will pay
two sestertii for the day." Maeli tried to do the
calculations in her head the way Aeran did.
She agreed quickly and Marcus finished his
food before heading to his cubiculum.

Maired was cleaning up the dishes as
she saw Marcus walk from his cubiculum to
the bathhouse door. Eòin had been waiting in
case he wanted a bath and led the young man
into the bathhouse. Maired had to focus on
her task, so she didn't think of him wearing
that toga.

As the sun went down, Maired kept
hoping her mother would head to bed early.
Maeli spent time in the tabiculum to see if she
would end up making much profit. As Maired
looked in on her she could tell her mother
was frustrated with how the calculations were
coming out. She would have to figure out
how to make two sestertii cover the costs.

Marcus had gone back to his room
and there was light from his lamp spilling out
from under the door. Maired was working
hard to find more chores to keep busy until
her mother went to bed. Finally, she went up
the stairs, Maired followed to make it appear
she was going to sleep too. She changed into a

clean under tunic and got into bed. She lay
there and listened to her mother move around
in the other room.

All was silent. Maired waited, wanting
to be sure her mother was asleep. She snuck
over to the door to her mother's room and
whispered out to her but got no response.
Content that she was asleep, Maired quietly
went down the stairs, through the lichen and
into the courtyard. There was still light
coming from under Marcus' door.

Maired knocked on the door, it
opened and Marcus stood there wearing
nothing but his white subligaculum. Maired
was a little nervous but stepped into his room.

Chapter 10
Taran

Taran woke, enjoying the soft rocking of a boat on a calm sea. He lay in bed in the dark berth of the ship that had given him passage from Gaza to Gaul. He looked down at the dark hair spread across his chest. Samira was snuggled up close so they could both fit on this small bunk. He put his arm around her and pulled her in, the feel of her skin against his was an unexpected bonus to being married.

They had joined together in marriage in her father's tent, sharing a feast to celebrate the agreement. Malik had given Taran a traditional Nabatean robe to wear, which he wore with pride. They made a formal agreement to share their wealth, business and family. They had one night together in a tent, before getting on board the ship.

They had switched ships in Gaul, and this ship was headed to Londinium. They would remove their cargo in town and Pyrros had offered to manage the sale of the oil and spices so he could introduce Samira to his parents. As they came up on deck, they could see the port of Londinium up ahead. This was always a sight that he enjoyed seeing, it meant a successful end to his journey.

Taran helped unload the cargo and made sure he and Pyrros agreed on a good price. He trusted Pyrros to get a better price if he could. He would then join them at the Caupona Caureni to split the profits and plan their next journey.

The city felt more like Rome than a part of Brittania. Taran hadalways enjoyed visiting as a child. It felt to him like leaving his home country and traveling to another place. He would often seek out travelers to learn about different destinations.

Now he was able to introduce his wife to the great city. After getting the merchandise stored in a warehouse close to the docks, they went out to explore the city. They would leave for Caerwyn early in the morning. They visited the market and the forum. Samira was impressed by the columns and the sheer size of the market. Thousands of people trading and doing business made her excited at the prospect of making money.

The next morning, they hired a wagon to take them to Caerwyn. The journey would take all day, Samira enjoyed looking at the roundhouses, with their thatch roofs and short walls. Her only complaint was about the cold; Samira spent her life in the desert. Brittania, on its warmest day was still cold for her. Taran had bought her a wool dress and cloak. With her gold earrings and bracelets, the wool dress looked out of place.

It was almost sunset when the caupona came into sight. Taran stood in the wagon with excitement and pointed it out to Samira. She was nervous to meet Taran's parents. Taran had told her the story of how his parents had met when his father had rescued her from the slave market. She respected a man that treated women with dignity.

The archway, the entrance to home, stood just as Taran remembered it. They got out of the wagon and walked through the arch. Taran was surprised to find that nobody was in the courtyard. It was never this quiet. Samira followed him in and looked around; she was impressed with the neat tables and open kitchen with the roaring fire.

"You have a well right in your home?" Samira asked. For someone whose life revolved around finding clean water, this was the most luxurious thing she had seen.

"Yes," Taran said, looking at the stone wall that surrounded the well. It seemed normal to him; it was interesting to see his home through someone else's eyes. "It's so quiet. I wonder if something is happening in town." He saw a flash of red coming down the stairs. Maired came into the kitchen and looked at them.

"Taran!" Maired shouted. She ran into his arms and squealed in joy. The shout brought Maeli rushing down the stairs as well. She ran to her son and hugged him. Maeli then saw the two strangers who were with him.

"Who are these two?" Maeli asked.

"This is Gaius," Taran started with the easy introduction, "he's a friend I met in Petra. And this," Taran took Samira's hand "this is Samira. My wife." Maeli gasped and Maired squealed.

"Your wife?" Maeli asked.

"Yes," Taran said, "we just got married. She's from near Petra." Taran looked around the courtyard expectantly, "where's Da? I want him to meet her." Both Maeli and Maired's faces fell.

"Come," Maeli said, "sit in the kitchen, I have to tell you something." Taran's heart stopped. He knew it couldn't be good news. He walked with his mother to the kitchen and sat at the table. Maired went to get some ale for everyone. Samira slowly walked behind, sensing trouble.

"What's going on?" Taran asked.

"Your father got sick shortly after you left," Maeli said. "He's gone son." Taran sat quietly for a moment. He didn't know what to think. His father was his best friend growing up, teaching him how to barter and be a good businessman. Samira sat beside him and took his hand. He barely felt her hand in his.

"I can't believe it," Taran said, "he's really gone?"

"Oh, my love," Samira said in the Nabatean tongue, "to lose a father is a great sorrow." Maeli and Maired looked at them, amazed. They were more amazed when Taran responded.

"He has become part of the land," Taran said to Samira, "this is our belief."

"It is a good belief," Samira said.

"Such an exotic sounding language," Maeli said softly. "Does she speak Latin?"

"Yes Domina," Samira said politely, "I'm sorry, in my sorrow for your loss I forget." Taran smiled at his wife.

"She's Nabatean," Taran said, still looking at Samira. "They are travelers."

"That's perfect for you!" Maired exclaimed. "Those armbands are so pretty." Samira looked at her bracelets and took one off.

"It is yours," Samira said, handing the bracelet to Maired. Maired took it and turned it over in her hands. It was gold and had intricate designs carved into it.

"Thank you," Maired said.

"That was kind," Maeli said. "Why don't you get settled, we will visit later."

"If there is a room available for Gaius," Taran said, "that would be good. Samira and I can share my old bed."

"All the rooms are empty," Maeli said, "we have lost all business." Taran was a little taken aback, more bad news.

"We will get settled and after that I will build a fire and we can talk," Taran said. He took Gaius to the nicest room, close to the bathhouse. He and Samira took the next room. Once they had all their luggage sorted Taran built a fire in the courtyard.

Maeli joined him sitting at the fire and the two talked late into the night. Maeli told Taran about the last few weeks of his father's life. How he had constantly bragged about his son who was a successful trader. Taran shared memories of his father and the two mourned quietly together.

Taran would still need time to mourn, but this time with his mother was the best way to start the mourning process. He stayed by the fire after his mother went to bed and remembered his father. He allowed himself a moment, when nobody was around to weep. When he finally went to his bed he felt like he could move on.

The next morning Taran woke late and found his wife in the kitchen, helping prepare the morning meal. He walked over to join them, Samira saw him and waved.

"Before you come," Samira called, "please bring water from the well." Taran chuckled to himself as he drew the water, she hadn't taken long to feel at home. He could see his mother smiling. As Taran delivered the bucket of water to Samira, Maeli put an arm around his shoulder and kissed his cheek.

"She insisted we put her to work," Maeli said.

"Of course she did," Taran said, "Samira likes to keep busy." Taran helped with getting the food on the table. Gaius joined them as they were sitting down at the table.

"Mother," Taran said as Gaius sat. "I forgot to tell you; Gaius is a follower of the teachings of Iēsus." Maeli's face lit up when he said that. She had read the letter from Paulus so many times but still didn't fully understand it. She knew there had to be more she could learn.

"Welcome," Maeli said, "I'm sure Taran told you of the codex we have."

"Yes Domina," Gaius said, "I am anxious to read it. I have a codex I can share

in exchange. It is the writing of a man called
Marcus. It's the account of the life of Iēsus."

"I would like to read that," Maeli said.
Taran knew his mother would get on well
with Gaius. On the journey Gaius had
explained some of the teaching of Iēsus, but
Taran had not read the scroll yet. He was
happy Gaius had decided to come. He looked
around the courtyard, it was so empty.

"Why are there no guests?" Taran
asked abruptly.

"We don't know" Maeli said. "People
just stopped coming a month or so after your
father died." Taran shook his head. That
didn't make sense, Caupona Caureni had
stood here for generations. He would have to
ask around to figure out what was happening.

After eating, Maeli rushed to get the
codex to show it to Gaius. Taran decided to
head to the village, he had some friends there
he could talk to. He wanted to introduce them
to Samira as well.

The village of Caerwyn wasn't very
big, a small market, a great house for meetings
and a few roundhouses where people
conducted business. The leather worker had a
small shop, and the blacksmith shop was
outside of the village.

In the market there was a small booth
where spices were sold. It was run by a man

named Ivor, who was a good friend of Taran. Taran had a small selection of spices to sell to him, so this was his first stop.

"Taran!" Ivor said as he saw his friend. "It's been a long time."

"It has," Taran said, giving his friend a hug. "I want you to meet Samira, my wife." Ivor and Samira exchanged polite greetings as Taran pulled out the spices he had brought. Ivor's face lit up.

"I see you have brought me treasure!" Ivor said.

"Costly treasure," Taran teased. He handed the spices over, and Ivor inspected the seals on the packages and opened some to smell them.

"A denarius for the lot?" Ivor said hopefully. Taran smiled and shook his head.

"Add two sestertii to that," Taran said, this was still low, but he wanted something else. "And some information."

"Deal," Ivor said, "depending on what information you need." He was already counting the coins.

"Do you know why my father's Caupona is sitting empty?" Taran asked. Ivor looked around and lowered his voice.

"Word is," Ivor said softly, "your mother is selling information to the Romans.

It doesn't help that the Romans are now using it as a headquarters." This was news to Taran.

"My mother?" Taran asked, "she barely tolerates the Romans. She would never sell information to them." Ivor shrugged.

"Just saying what I've heard," Ivor said. Taran took his coins and thanked Ivor before heading to the great house. There were often elders sitting around the entrance talking about the old times. He explained to Samira that the great house held a long table used for feasts and ceremonies. It was the social hub of the village.

The long building with the thatched roof and mud daubed walls was getting old. It had stood here as long as Taran could remember. There were a few men sitting out front. One of them was Garan the white, named so for his white beard and hair. He was a grizzled old man with deep wrinkles and a stern look. He had been old as far back as Taran could remember.

"Garan!" Taran called out as they approached, "how is the weather?"

"Cold and wet!" Garan said sternly.

"My wife agrees," Taran said with a smile.

"You finally found a woman?" Garan said, "she is smart if she agrees with Old Garan. How did you convince her to marry you?" Taran laughed and slapped the old man's knee. Garan looked at Samira and his eyes got bigger. "She's a beautiful girl."

"Thank you," Samira said, bowing slightly out of respect for the man. Ivor enjoyed the respect and it showed. He sat up a little straighter and smiled.

"Garan," Taran said, "I'm hearing rumors about my mother."

"I've heard them too," Garan said, "it's all nonsense, but you youngsters believe everything you're told." Taran shook his head.

"How can we convince people of the truth?" Taran asked.

"I don't know," Garan said, "people are forgetful, in a month they will be telling a new story, I am sure." Taran smiled and thanked the old man. To his surprise Samira pulled a small knife from her skirt and handed it to Garan. It had an ornate handle and well-tooled leather sheath.

"For you," Samira said, "a thank you for your wisdom." Garan took it and turned it over.

"You can bring your wife to visit anytime," Garan said with a smile. Taran took her hand as they walked away. He was proud of how well she was able to win people over.

Chapter 11
Maired

Maired had one more job to do before she would be given the freedom to run in the woods. She planned to invite Samira this time. As she hung the laundry on the line, she looked at her bracelet. It caught the light and glistened back at her. She was so happy that Taran had married such a wonderful person. She quickly finished and rushed off to find Samira.

As she entered the courtyard, she saw Marcus coming through the arch. She hadn't seen him since that night they spent together. She greeted him as politely as she could and escorted him to the kitchen, where her mother was cooking.

"Domina," Marcus said, "I have been sent to make arrangements for another meeting."

"Very good," Maeli said, "do you have the number of people coming?"

"Not yet," Marcus said, "I will go to give out invitations."

"We will have your room ready," Maeli said and the boy rushed off to conduct his business. Maeli sent Maired off to prepare the only empty room. It was the one closest to the entryway, which meant she could easily

come again tonight. If she crept along the
wall, nobody would be able to see her.

As Maired prepared the room her
mind went back to the last night they had
been together. Maired had not expected to be
so intimate, but she had hoped that they
might. He had not been forceful but had led
her to her own decision to give herself to him.
She longed for his touch again. She was still
daydreaming when she came out of the room
and nearly walked into Taran.

"You seem happy," Taran said.
Maired had not realized she had been smiling.

"We have another guest," Maired said,
"he's from the Roman camp nearby." Taran
wondered if this was part of what people had
been talking about.

"Has he been here before?" Taran
asked.

"Yes," Maired said, "he sets up
meetings with people from town."

"What are the meetings for?" Taran
asked, trying not to become agitated.

"Just meetings," Maired responded
with a shrug. Maired rushed off to head to the
woods. She wondered why Taran seemed
upset about the meetings. They needed
customers. She thought about inviting Samira
along but then remembered that Marcus
might show up.

Maired rushed through the woods to the clearing as fast as she could. Marcus was there, laying in the tall grass staring at the sky. She quietly came up to him.

"What are you looking at?" Maired asked with a giggle.

"You!" Marcus said as he gently pulled her on top of himself. Maired squealed with delight as she found herself being pulled into his arms. He kissed her and put his arms around her, pulling her tight. The kiss lasted a while and when Maired lifted her head she moved off to the side of Marcus. Maired lay there with her hand on his chest, she could feel his muscles, Maired sighed in contentment.

"I'm glad you're back," Maired said.

"My father told me last night," Marcus said, "I haven't slept all night thinking about you. Have you been thinking about me?"

"Every day," Maired said.

"That's good," Marcus said, he moved his hand to her lower back, rubbing it gently. He kept moving lower on her back, but Maired enjoyed his touch.

"My brother and his wife are staying in the room next to yours," Maired said.

"So you won't be coming to my room tonight?" Marcus sounded sad with this question. He moved his hand to her shoulder.

"I'm just saying we need to be careful." Maired said, using her hand to move his hand lower again.

"Absolutely," Marcus said with a smile. He rolled so they were facing each other and they started kissing again. Marcus was much less annoying when he was kissing her. Maired loved the feeling of him touching her.

Maired lost all track of time and finally realized how late it had gotten. She got up and readjusted her dress as she rushed off to get back home. She hoped her mother wouldn't be too upset. Fortunately, her mother was busy as she snuck through the arch. Maired quickly went to the well and started to bring up water.

The rest of the afternoon was busy enough that Maired didn't have to talk to anyone. She went through her day, thinking about Marcus. When he came in, she made sure he had everything he needed, imagining to herself they were married already and she was taking care of her husband.

Unfortunately, since Gaius was a paying guest, he sat with Marcus at mealtime and the two spent the time talking. Marcus kept looking her way, but she couldn't really sit with them. Her mother wouldn't allow it. Samira caught her looking at him.

"He's handsome," Samira said, indicating Marcus.

"Yes," Maired said.

"Be careful of handsome men," Samira said. Maired noticed Taran was close behind her and seemed to be listening in.

"Is that why you are with my brother?" Maired said loud enough for Taran to hear.

"He's brave," Taran said, "he fought many bandits in the desert." Maired looked at her brother, she never imagined him fighting bandits.

"You killed a few yourself," Taran said, standing behind her and wrapping his arms around her waist. Maired looked at his brother and his wife in awe.

"What happened," Maired asked.

"Bandits were shooting our caravan with arrows," Taran said. "Samira's father sent us, her brother and some other men to fight them. "We crawled across the desert floor and found them and killed them."

"Your brother showed his skill as a warrior," Samira said. Maired shook her head in disbelief.

"I thought you were a trader," Maired said.

"Traders are a little bit of everything," Taran said. "We need to be able to fight the

bandits, barter the prices, manage the money."
Maired looked out at the courtyard. She had
met many traders as a girl; they had come to
her courtyard. She never realized what kind of
lives those men led.

Marcus and Gaius finished their food
and Maired started cleaning up the dishes. She
watched across the courtyard as the men
walked over to the bathhouse. She tried to
keep her mind occupied on her tasks instead
of thinking about Marcus.

The sun finally set and people slowly
went to their beds. Maired lay in her bed until
all was quiet. She snuck across the courtyard,
staying in the shadows of the wall. She had
wrapped her cloak around her, if caught she
would say she was going to the latrīna.

Marcus had left his door open a crack,
so Maired didn't need to knock. He was
already in his bed; a lantern still lit on the
table. Maired quietly closed the door and
doused the lamp before sliding off her cloak
and under tunic. She slid into bed next to
Marcus and kissed him.

Later that night, Maired got dressed
and quietly opened the door. She looked out
but saw nobody. She moved across to the
wall, trying to keep in the shadows. As she
came into the kitchen she sighed in relief. She
had made it. She started for the stairs and was

startled to see Samira standing at the base of the stairs, her arms crossed on her chest.

"Samira!" Maired said in surprise, "can I help you?"

"No," Samira sounded upset. "I come to get water. I see you coming from that boy's room." She was struggling to find the words; she was very upset.

"I was using the Latrīna," Maired said, trying the ruse she had come up with.

"The Latrīna is not in a boy's room," Samira was not fooled, Maired wasn't sure what she would do next.

"I was in there with Marcus," she confessed. "Please don't tell."

"You are not married to him," Samira said sternly. "Has he promised marriage?"

"Not really," Maired said softly. "We are just, he's just," Maired trailed off, not knowing what to say.

"He's using you," Samira said. "I think he should marry you." Maired wondered about that. Did she want to marry Marcus? She liked spending time with him, but only when they were kissing. Otherwise, he was annoying.

"I don't think of him like that," Maired said, "please don't tell anyone."

"It is late," Samira said, "I will not wake your brother. If you stop with this boy, I will keep your secret." Maired smiled.

"Thank you," she wrapped her arms around Samira and kissed her cheek.

Chapter 12
Taran

Taran watched the men gather for the meeting. He was told they would be merchants and traders from the village, he knew some of them and they were farmers. When the Centurion arrived, he had introduced himself, hoping to be invited.

Gaius walked through the courtyard as they were talking and paused, listening to the Centurion. They hadn't noticed him at first but stopped talking when they saw him. He smiled and walked over to the group. The group stayed silent as he approached. He bent over and drew something in the dust on the ground.

Taran stretched to see what it was; it looked like a fish. The Centurion smiled and invited Gaius to join them. After the meeting, Gaius brought the Centurion over to where Maeli was standing.

"Maeli," Gaius said, "there is a group of believers here!" Maeli looked as confused as Taran felt. "The Centurion, Quintus, is a follower of Iēsus. He is meeting here because he doesn't want anyone in the camp to know."

"It would end my career," Quintus said, "maybe even my life." Gaius nodded,

Taran realized that Gaius had run because of
his belief in Iēsus. He had read some of Gaius
scroll about Iēsus teaching and understood
why.

The Emperor Domitian was
considered to be a god. Iēsus taught that there
was one God, the Judean God. A Roman
Centurion would definitely be risking his life
by denying the Emperor's deity.

"We will keep your secret," Maeli said,
"you are welcome to meet here as often as
you'd like." Taran wondered how he could let
people know these meetings were innocent.

"We do have one small problem,"
Taran said. "The Britons think you are here to
spy on them. And that we are feeding you
information." Quintus stoked his chin, he
recognized how serious that was.

"I see," Quintus said, "I didn't mean
to cause you harm. There are followers in the
village, we will find a way to restore your
reputation." Taran wasn't sure they could but
was happy they wanted to try.

Pyrros arrived later that day after the
followers of Iēsus had gone. He brought
Taran his share of the profits. Taran knew he
needed to save some of this money for his
next trip. He also had an idea.

Taran spent the next week traveling to
Londinium and purchasing everything he

needed. When he arrived back at the inn, he sent out invitations to help him celebrate his marriage. A public celebration, with no information being shared, should bring people in. Help them forget their suspicions.

The day of the celebration came quickly. The first person to arrive was Garan. He was wearing the knife he had been given proudly on his belt.

"Young man," Garan said, "I am honored to be the first to have met your exotic wife." Taran handed him some ale and he drank. "I forgot how good your ale is." Garan went to greet Maeli as more people came in.

The celebration had a great turnout as people were excited to meet the exotic woman in their midst. Samira dressed in her most elegant dress, flowing silk with an embroidered head scarf. She wrapped it neatly around her head, leaving her big earrings showing. She had even put a small gem in her nose piercing. The people were amazed that someone from so far away would be in their small inn.

Chapter 13
Samira

The plan had worked. Within a week Taran and Samira had moved into the family quarters, taking Maeli's room. Gaius had offered to give up his room and moved into the old slave quarters with Eòin. People were visiting for meals and travelers were spending the night again.

Samira found it amusing how quickly her husband fell into the role of innkeeper. She enjoyed the role she had now as well. She had taken over the kitchen, preparing traditional Nabatean dishes along with local cuisine. Her exotic food was a favorite and travelers spread the word.

She was in the kitchen with Maeli, going over the supplies they had left. Plotting to send Taran off on a supply run. Maired came back to the kitchen from the latrīna, looking a little green. Maeli watched her go and shook her head.

"Poor thing," Maeli said, "she was sick yesterday morning as well." Samira thought about that. She had not shared Maired's secret but was wondering if it would still come out on it's own. She excused herself and joined Maired at the well.

"You are sick?" Samira asked. Maired had been bent at the waist washing her face with the cool water. She looked up at Samira.

"I don't know," Maired said, "I vomited yesterday morning but felt fine later." Samira shook her head sadly.

"Has your," Samira stopped for a moment, she was trying to say something she didn't know the words for. "Have you had blood?" Samira pointed at Maired's groin, "down there?" Maired looked at Samira blankly, this was a very personal question. She had started her monthly a few years back but had never really talked to anyone about it.

"Yes," Maired said sternly, "I have my monthly's." Samira sighed in relief. She realized it had been too soon since she caught Maired with the boy. She didn't need to worry. Maired walked off quickly and felt her stomach get upset again.

Samira watched her rush to the latrīna again, wondering if the time she had caught Maired had been the first time. She quietly followed Maired and stood by the door to the latrīna. After the sound of heaving was finished, she could hear the girl weeping. Samira knocked on the door and walked in.

Maired was sitting on the floor, tears flowing down her cheeks. Samira lifted her and carried her to an empty stall in the stable.

She lay Maired gently in the hay and sat next to her. Maired put her head on Samira's lap and sniffed, trying to stop crying. After a moment she looked up at Samira.

"My monthly hasn't come in a over a month," Maired said softly. Samira ran her hand along the girl's head, smoothing her hair. It was as Samira had expected. The girl was with child. She sighed and sat quietly and let Maired have a moment.

"You have been with that boy before that night?" Samira asked, Maired nodded gently.

"I didn't even think about it until you asked," Maired said, her voice shaky. "You think I'm going to have a baby?"

"I think that is what happens when you are alone with a boy," Samira said. Maired started to tear up again. Samira held her until she managed to calm down.

"What am I going to do?" Maired asked.

"You are going to go to your mother," Samira said. "She is a good person." Maired sniffed again. She obviously didn't want to talk to her mother. "I'll stay with you if you want."

"No," Maired said, sniffing, "I need to tell her." Maired slowly stood up and brushed the straw from her dress. She walked towards the kitchen, dreading what her mother would say. Samira walked with her to encourage her.

"Ma," Maired said softly, "can we talk, upstairs?" Maeli looked at her daughter and sensed something was wrong. The two walked up the stairs and Samira took a knife and started cutting some meat for a stew she had planned to cook. She knew the exact moment Maired confessed her wrongdoing as there was a loud exclamation from the family quarters.

Taran heard it from where he was standing with a guest, bartering the final charges. He looked over at Samira with a questioning look. She indicated that everything was all right. He finished his business and put the coins in the tabiculum before joining Samira.

"Do you know what happened?" Taran asked.

"I do," Samira said, "but maybe better you hear from them." Taran gave her a look and walked quietly up the stairs. Maired was laying on her bed weeping and Maeli was pacing the room angrily.

"Ma?" Taran asked. "What is wrong?"

"She," Maeli pointed at Maired, "has been intimate with a boy. And now she tells me she is with child!" Taran felt his blood rush to his ears. He stormed over to Maired and grabbed her wrist.

"Who?" Taran demanded, "who did this to you?" Maired cried out and Taran glared at her angrily. Gently Samira came into the room and put her hand on Taran's hand.

"She's suffering enough," Samira said, "don't make it worse." Taran took a deep breath and tried to calm himself. He released his sister and walked away from her. Samira sat with Maired and held her close.

"I need to find the boy," Taran said, "he will marry her and take care of her and the child."

"What if I don't want to?" Maired asked.

"You don't want to marry the boy you laid with?" Taran asked incredulously. Maired buried her head in Samira's shoulder. Samira raised a hand to help Taran focus.

"He is right child," Samira said calmly, "this is his child and he needs to be responsible. By being with him, you chose him."

"I didn't think," Maired started.

"You're right," Maeli interrupted, "you didn't think." Maeli sat on a stool and sighed. "We need to know who it is Maired." Maired looked at Samira, who nodded gently to encourage her.

"I can't" Maired said. "I don't want to marry him!" She collapsed into tears again. Samira realized that she needed to do something but wasn't sure what best to do. She didn't want to betray this new sister, but she had an obligation to her husband. She stood up and walked over to Taran.

"I know who it is," Samira said, "I saw her leaving the room of that Roman boy." Taran's face grew red.

"Why didn't you tell me?" Taran asked.

"She asked me not to," Samira said gently. Taran was angry, but he could see in his wife's eyes that she had been in a hard situation. Stuck in a culture she didn't understand, dealing with a family she didn't know.

"Tell me everything," Taran said sternly.

"I was returning from the latrīna late one night," Samira started. "I saw her returning from the boy's room. I did not ask what they had done, but now it is obvious."

"I wish you had told me," Taran said in Nabatean, "but it was a difficult situation. You are a part of the family now and must make decisions as a sister and a wife."

"I will remember I am a wife first," Samira said. Taran looked at his sister, lying on the bed dejected and his mother was pacing again.

"I think she needs a sister now," Taran said. "I'll be back," Taran rushed from the room.

"Where is he going?" Maired asked.

"Probably to talk to the boy's father," Maeli said. Samira left the mother and daughter and went down the stairs in time to see her husband rushing out the archway.

Chapter 14
Taran

The walk to the Roman camp took a little over an hour, which gave Taran some time to calm himself a little. He had to be careful about approaching a Centurion about the misdeeds of his son. It was best to be calm. The green hills, covered with farmers' fields, helped calm him. The camp was located on the top of a tall hill, and Taran was mostly calm by the time he climbed the hill.

The camp was surrounded by a ditch and a small wooden fence. There were many tents organized in rows visible beyond the gate. Taran approached the guard; a legionary dressed in full armor with a small pilum rested on his shoulder.

"Good morning," Taran said pleasantly, "I am Taranus Lupinus," he used the name his father had taught him to use when dealing with Romans. Lupinus was the name his grandfather was given in Rome, and his father had passed it on to him. "I am looking for Centurion Quintus Tiberius." The guard called a runner to fetch the Centurion's aide. Before long Taran saw the same boy who had come to the caupona before the Centurion's visit.

"Yes?" the boy asked politely.

"I need to speak with the Centurion," Taran said sternly.

"Come with me," the boy said, he was obviously proud of his ability to give people access to the camp. They walked down the row of tanned leather tents. After seeing the woven hair tents of the desert, they looked hot and uncomfortable. They approached a slightly larger tent at the end of one of the rows. This one had a red flag outside with the image of a gold bull painted on it.

"Centurion," the boy said at the entrance to the tent, "the master of the Caupona Caureni."

"Enter," came a deep voice from inside the tent. The boy lifted a flap and stood aside so Taran could enter. The inside was dark, but spacious. There were two low beds and a table at one end where Quintus sat. Two legionaries stood with him at the table.

"Thank you for seeing me," Taran said, "I am here on personal business." Taran looked pointedly at the men at the table. Quintus dismissed them with a word. The boy left too.

"Is this about our meetings?" Quintus asked quietly, "if so, I ask you to speak quietly."

"No," Taran said, "I am coming to discuss your son's relationship with my sister."

"Your sister?" Quintus asked, "the girl with the red hair? I was not aware there was any relationship."

"They have been intimate," Taran said softly, successfully hiding his anger that was still churning inside.

"That is a strong accusation," Quintus said, do you have any evidence?

"She is with child," Taran said. Quintus started to speak and Taran quickly added "and my wife saw her leaning his room during his last stay." Quintus' face fell. He could not argue against that. He sent for Marcus who came quickly.

"What is your relationship with the sister of this caupo," Quintus asked, indicating Taran. Marcus looked over at Taran and shook his head gently.

"I have spoken with her," Marcus said, "but nothing more."

"She was seen leaving your room," Quintus said sternly.

"I'm sure she was bringing me some ale," Marcus said. "That is her job." Taran was impressed by his composure, even if he was certain it was all a lie. Quintus looked to

Taran, but by his expression Taran knew Quintus was not certain what to believe.

"My wife said it was after everyone was in bed," Taran said accusingly. Marcus looked at the floor and shook his head again.

"A lie," Marcus said. "I wouldn't do anything with that cauponaria!" It took all he had to keep his anger at bay.

"She is carrying your child," Taran said through gritted teeth. The boy lifted his head and grinned.

"She is?" Marcus asked excitedly. "I'm going to be a father?" Quintus' head snapped to look at his son. Taran felt some satisfaction; the boy was too young to keep the ruse when surprised.

"You admit you are the child's father?" Quintus asked. Marcus' face fell quickly, realizing he had given himself up.

"Yes, father," Marcus said. Quintus asked Taran to step out of the tent. Taran obliged, stepping through the flap into the world of the Roman military. He wondered about making his sister marry that boy.

It was the right thing to do, and the only way to protect her honor. He wondered why she objected to marrying him. He knew people that had married people they didn't like in arranged marriages. It was rare, but it happened. Why would she get into a physical relationship with someone she didn't like?

He caught some of what the Centurion was saying to the boy, and none of it was pleasant. Taran was angry with the boy and was gratified that the boy's father felt the same. After a few minutes Taran was called back in.

"Will you be willing to allow your sister to marry this boy?" Quintus asked quietly. Taran could tell he was seething. Taran briefly considered saying no, but realized that as unfortunate as it was, they needed to protect her reputation.

"I am," Taran said. He thought maybe they would grow to love each other, once this boy matures.

"Good," Quintus said. "I would not want my grandchild to be left without family. Come, let us drink together and discuss arrangements."

Part II

Escape the present
1 Year later

Chapter 15
Riva

Riva sat in the ruins of her roundhouse. The battle had been rough and long. Most of the men of the clan were dead, including her husband and her father. Her son was missing and all she had left was a broken sword and the clothes on her back. She thought about using the sword to finish her suffering.

"If you're thinking of hurting yourself," a deep voice behind her said, "don't." Riva turned to see her older brother Cyn standing where the door used to be. She jumped up and wrapped her arms around him. He wasn't her biological brother; her mother had found him in a burned-out village when he was small. Riva had grown up considering him a brother.

Cyn stood a little taller than she was, compared to most men he was short. He didn't spend much time with people, his dark hair was always unkempt, and his clothes had been patched many times. He didn't like the feel of a beard, so he kept it shaved off.

"They're all dead, Da, Eiran, all of them," Riva said. She buried his head into her chest. Eiran had not been the best husband, but he had been hers. Cyn held her for a moment.

"Artor's alive," Cyn said softly.

"I don't even know," Riva sobbed, "he might be."

"He is," Cyn said, "I

saw him leaving with raiders." Riva pulled back and looked at Cyn. Her dark blonde hair was falling into her face, and she had to pull it back to look into his eyes. They were the same dark brown color as her own, she saw hope in his eyes. Maybe Artor, her son, was still alive.

"Where?" Riva asked. Cyn put an arm around her shoulder and led her out of the remains of her roundhouse. The fallen thatch crinkling under their feet. The smell of smoke still lingered as they moved toward the southern edge of the village. Cyn pointed along the trail that headed south.

Cyn was not a talkative person, he had already said more to Riva today than he normally did. Growing up their Ma joked that Riva spoke enough for the two of them. When their mother died, Cyn moved into the forest and lived off the land. He visited Riva and their father but kept to himself most of the time.

Riva looked along the trail and wondered what to do. She knew she had to get her son back, but she didn't know where to start. Her father was the warrior, her brother was the hunter, her husband was the one that thought everything through. All she had left was her brother. Cyn gently led her away from the path and into the forest.

They walked quietly through the forest, Riva tried to think of a plan as she walked. The attack on the village had come without warning before the sun had risen. Everything had happened so fast. Eiran had rushed to help the men defending the clan and Riva had hidden in her roundhouse with Artor.

The sounds of swords and shields clashing rang through the small village the clan had built near the river. A man had smashed through her door with an axe. She remembered everything about him. His head brushed against the roof; he wore a bronze helmet that protected his nose. He had a short beard and long hair. He had found her and Artor hiding behind a blanket they had hanging from the roof.

He had smiled, when he saw Riva, his teeth were crooked. He got close to her, so close she could smell his breath. Fear ran through her, wondering what he was planning. Then he saw Artor. His face softened and he picked the boy up and rushed out. Riva chased after him, but he hit her so hard she fell back and felt the world go black. The last thing she heard was her son calling for her.

As they walked, Riva tried to focus on what she could do. Artor was her whole life, ever since he had been born three years ago. She was just too tired, too stressed, too emotional to think. Cyn led her on gently, helping her over fallen trees and around rocks as they walked away from the death.

Cyn brought Riva to a cave entrance that was low to the ground. Riva didn't even see it until they were climbing down towards it. Its arched entrance was so small they had to bend to get through. Once they were through the cave opened up and they could stand. Riva did notice that they had to step around a small hearth made by placing rocks in a circle.

Inside the cave, Cyn lit a small clay lamp, and in the dim light Riva could see a small bed made with tree boughs and blankets. There were a few rocks outcroppings that held clay jars. She realized this was where Cyn must be living.

"Welcome," Cyn said as he put the lamp on a rock shelf and started to collect some dry wood from a pile by his bed. He walked back to the entrance and built up the fire. Before long the cave was warming up and felt a little more comfortable.

"This is your home?" Riva asked. Cyn nodded and pointed to the bed.

"Rest," Cyn said. Riva lay down and closed her eyes. Cyn watched her sleep, he would do anything for Riva, his only family left.

Chapter 16
Maired

The baby was crying again. Maired got out of bed and took the baby from his cradle. Lupinus was only a few months old but controlled every aspect of Maired's life, even sleep. She picked the boy up and sat on a stool to nurse him.

She looked at the boy; he had red hair like her but otherwise he looked just like his father, Maired resented that. This child that ruined her life, didn't even have the decency to look like her.

Shortly after being married to Marcus, the Centurion Quintus sent them to Rome. They were given a room in the domus of a relative of Quintus. She never understood the exact relationship between them, just that she was expected to keep the baby in the room and stay out of the way.

Maired looked around her small room, she had her bed, that she sometimes shared with Marcus. When he was home. A table with reclinium so she could eat. A cradle for the baby and a mat in the corner where Litana was sleeping.

Litana was a slave from the household, she was about fourteen or fifteen years old. Her dark hair was curly and hard to manage. Her large brown eyes spoke of innocence and her little nose always crinkled when she was asked to change the baby's soiled clothes. She wasn't the brightest child and had to be taught how to do the same task several times.

Marcus had been sworn in as a legionary now and Maired had to admit he looked handsome in his armor. The shiny metal plates across his chest, red tunic and shiny arm bands made him look so official. He was gone, assigned to his father's regiment back in Briton. She had pleaded to be allowed go with him, but he told her things were not done that way.

Now it was just her and the baby and a slow slave that didn't understand half of what was going on. Maired sighed as the baby stopped nursing and went back to sleep. She put him into his cradle and lay back in her bed. Maybe she could get a few more hours of sleep before the baby cried again.

The morning came too soon and Maired was woken by Litana. She was smiling at Maired in a way that infuriated her. What did she have to be happy about? Maired sat up and Litana walked over to the table.

"I got the food," Litana said. This was her first job of the day, fetching the small allotment of food Maired received from her patron. Slowly getting out of bed, Maired noticed that today she had some cold meat on her table. She wondered what had happened in order for her to get such a treat. Maired ate some of the bread and meat and set the rest of the food aside for later.

"I think today we should go to town," Maired said. Litana smiled, she liked town. Maired had received her monthly allowance from Marcus. He sent a denarius every month. Maired would usually buy herself a hot meal in town and then save the rest, she had counted the coins the night before and had enough now to buy herself a dress. She felt like a barbarian in her old clothes. Roman fashion was much more refined and beautiful.

After eating, Litana got the baby dressed while Maired got herself ready. The room had a private entrance; it was close to the main entrance of the domus. Maired could come and go without anyone noticing. The domus was nestled in with others in this small community. The roads were constantly busy, Maired tried to blend in, but her clothes and red hair made that difficult.

Litana walked a step behind Maired, carrying the baby. The stone buildings on either side of the street towered over them blocking the sun. The air was thick and filled with smoke and the smell of the dirty water in the gutters of the street. Maired thought back to her clearing in the woods. She missed the fresh air and sunlight.

The hot food was available at a small shop a short distance from the domus. Litana had shown it to her when she first arrived. The baby had not been born at that time and the walk was difficult. At least she had gotten her strength back quickly after the baby came. Since her patron did not believe in giving her hot food, this small shop was a real treat. Maired bought herself some hot lentil stew and treated Litana to a bowl as well.

"What are we doing next Domina?" Litana asked. The baby was asleep in her arms, it slept all the time, when it did wake it just lay there and looked around. Maired hoped she would love it, but it was just a burden.

"I want a dress. A Roman dress," Maired said. "I want to fit in."

"You're so beautiful," Litana said, "you think you will fit in?" Maired laughed, Litana often would say things in a way that amused her. The question made it sound like Litana felt she was so beautiful she wouldn't fit in.

"I'm going to try," Maired said, "after all, Marcus might become a general one day. I need to look like a general's wife." Maired laughed at her own little joke, but Litana gave her a nod. To Litana that made sense. Maired had little hope that her husband would become anything more than a legionary.

The dress shop had some beautiful dresses that had delicate embroidery and rich colors. Those were all too expensive. The lady helping Maired walked the back of the shop with her where she the simple dresses were kept. She helped Maired select a linen dress that flowed like water. It was a simple off white dress, but when Maired put it on she felt so pretty. It emphasized the curves that had become more prevalent after the baby.

Maired handed over her precious few coins and wore the dress out of the shop. Latira held the old dress over her free arm, the other arm still holding the baby. Maired walked down the street with confidence she hadn't felt in a year. As she walked men noticed her, she could see them turning their heads to appreciate her beauty. She was going to fit in now.

Chapter 17
Samira

Samira put the knife down and clutched her stomach. The pain was more regular. She wanted to finish getting the fish cut up before going and laying down. She had already scaled and cleaned the fish, all that remained was to cut it up and place it onto the clay pot that was already simmering on the fire. She finished quickly, the smell of the fish was almost overwhelming, and Samira longed to be still.

The first months of her pregnancy had been easy, she never felt sick. These last few weeks, any strong smell nauseated her. The pain came again; she was certain she would be holding her baby soon. She was certain it would be a girl, while Taran said it was a boy. It didn't really matter to Samira, but Taran wanted a son to take over the caupona one day.

The decision to stay had been difficult for Taran, he was a traveler at heart. His mother insisted he should maintain his trading lifestyle, but the loss of Maired had changed him. He had a responsibility as her elder brother and had done what needed to be done. Maeli had agreed with the decision, which helped. Maired, however, had begged not to be forced to marry.

Now Taran felt he needed to stay for his mother's sake. When Samira realized she was expecting, Taran had felt staying was the right thing. Got to the top of the stairs and felt the world turning. She carefully sat down on the top step and put her head in her hands.

"Are you alright?" Taran asked from the base of the stairs.

"I will be," Samira said, "once the baby is born." Taran came up the stairs and took his wife's hand. He helped her up and escorted her to their bed. There were two rooms up here, and Maeli had insisted they take the smaller, more private, room. This room had some shelves and a bed but was still more than anything Samira had while growing up. She was starting to enjoy life here. Taran had apologized that they might be stuck here, but there was always something to do. Life without sandstorms or bandits was also nice.

"Go get your mother," Samira said softly. Taran patted her hand and then rushed off. Samira took a deep breath as another pain came. She wondered what this child would be like, she would find out soon enough. As she lay there another pain came and then she felt a rush of water between her legs. She wanted

to move away from the wet spot but did not
have the energy.

"Taran says you need me," Marli said
as she entered the room.

"I think my water has come," Samira
said. Another pain came and took her breath
away. Maeli checked her dress and tutted.

"You poor thing," Maeli said, "we
need to get you cleaned up." Maeli helped
Samira sit up and remove her dress. She
helped her stand and put on a clean under
tunic before moving to the other room.
Samira reclined the bed and breathed deeply
to help control the pain.

Taran came through the doorway and
Maeli sent him off to fetch some warm water
and blankets. He rushed off excitedly. Maeli
shook her head and laughed.

"He's going to be useless for the next
few hours," Maeli said. Samira gave her a
small smile. The pain became more intense
over the next few minutes as Maeli held her
hand and gave her encouragement.

There was a small knock on the door,
and two more women came in, Seren and
Teleri had been beckoned. Maeli was happy to
see her husband's sister and niece arrive.
Taran had thought to send for them.

"What can we do?" Seren asked.

"I think I have everything now," Maeli said, "now we wait." Teleri had been over to help at the caupona often and Samira had learned to appreciate her quick wit and joy of life. Teleri sat on Samira's bed and started to tell a story about a cow that escaped from the fence. Her recounting the way her father and brother worked to get the cow back lightened the mood in the room.

They went through the afternoon talking and helping Samira walk around the room. As Teleri was lighting lamps because it was getting dark Samira felt that the pain had changed, feeling a little lower down. She shifted her weight; Seren had been holding her hand and realized something had changed.

"Did something happen?" Seren asked.

"The pain is lower," Samira said.

"Good," Seren said, "it is time to get up." Seren helped Samira get up and walk over to a table and stool they had set up for Samira. She used them to help support herself as she got into a squatting position. Seren told Teleri to stand behind Samira and support her.

The pain became more intense than anything Samira had ever felt. She felt a need to push, so she did. It was hard to stay in this position, but she stayed upright with the help of the three ladies. Her new family. A wave of emotions hit Samira. She was far from her mother, but these three women had become a fair substitute over the last year.

Maeli very cautiously checked between Samira's legs and announced that she could definitely see the top of the baby's head. Samira felt some relief that it should all be over soon. She could feel the warm hands of Teleri on her back and felt some comfort in that. Taking a deep breath, Samira pushed again. Maeli was watching for the baby and helped move it around a little.

Samira felt the baby move; it hurt but she knew it would be over soon. She pushed one more time and felt the baby almost fall away from her. Maeli gently pulled the baby up, and after a moment Seren tied the cord with a string and cut it with a very sharp knife.

"It's a girl!" Maeli said triumphantly as the baby started yelling. As Maeli wrapped the baby in a blanket, Samira felt something else come out. She looked down and saw the red blob of flesh. Seren told her that it was time to rest and helped her get to the bed.

Once settled, Maeli handed her the baby. Her daughter. She was still yelling, letting the world know that she was not happy. Samira put her to her breast, and the baby latched on and calmed down.

"She's a natural," Maeli said smiling, "her Da took a while to figure that out." Maeli turned to Teleri, "go tell Taran the baby is here, I'll come get him once we have it all cleaned up." Samira looked over to where Seren was cleaning up the blood that was on the floor.

"I am sorry," Sabrina said. Seren looked at her with a smile.

"It is no problem," Seren said, "all part of having babies." Sabrina looked down at her little girl. She and Taran had discussed naming the child, they had agreed that if it was a boy they would name him Aedan. Taran had told her that if it was a girl, she could find a name. The little girl turned and looked her mother in the eyes. She had pale brown eyes.

"I will call you Nura," Samira said softly, "my sun in this place where the clouds rule." Nura was the most beautiful girl Samira had ever seen. In that instant she knew she would do anything for this child. Before long she heard Taran coming up the stairs.

Taran slowly walked over and sat on the edge of the bed. Samira turned so he could see the baby and Nura could see her father.

"This is Nura," Samira said softly.

"She's beautiful," Taran said.

Chapter 18
Riva

The rain was gently falling on the leaves as Riva moved through the woods. She wrapped herself tightly in her cloak. As a child she loved days like this. She would run around in the rain until she was soaked through and then go into her home and remove all her wet clothes and sit by the fire without a stitch on. When he was younger Cyn would join her and the two would sit there giggling by the fire. They would stay there until their Ma yelled at them to get dressed.

Now there was no home and no hearth. Cyn was leading them to where he had last seen her son, Artor. The ground here was soft with all the rain, and there was a distinct trail of footprints from the group of raiders. Riva hoped to see a small footprint as evidence that her son had been among them, but that wasn't likely in this mess. There weren't many individual footprints, just a mess that told of many men walking through.

"I need a spear," Riva said, "or a sword." Cyn's look told her he wasn't understanding what she was thinking. "I'm going to rescue my son!" Riva exclaimed. She turned towards the field where the men had fought to keep the raiders from the village.

Surely there would be some weapons there amongst the dead.

Cyn followed closely as Riva came to the field. There were dead bodies lying all over. She slowly walked past the bodies of men she had known as far back as she could remember. Some of them were men she had grown up with. She didn't mourn; she didn't let herself feel anything. Until she saw Eiran's body.

He was lying face down in the mud, the back of his head covered in blood. Cyn helped her turn his body. His face was unharmed. She looked down at his slightly crooked nose and dark beard. She hadn't found him attractive, but she cared for him deeply. Not love as much as a deep fondness for him. She leaned down and gently kissed his blue lips, now cold and unfeeling. He had loved her; he told her he was the most fortunate man in the clan to be able to marry her.

His spear was by his side. Riva picked it up and looked at the shaft, it looked unharmed. She knew a man should be buried with his spear to take it to the other world, but she needed it. When Artor was born, Eiran had said he would give anything for his son. This would be his sacrifice, and Riva swore to him that his son would one day hold that spear.

Riva realized that Cyn was not beside her anymore. She looked around for him and spotted him on his knees beside another body. As she got closer, she realized that he had found their father. Cador the giant had finally been taken down by an enemy. His long grey beard with a single braid lay on his chest. Riva could imagine that he was just asleep, but knew he was gone as well. His spear was by his side, but the shaft was broken.

"We don't have time to bury you," she heard Cyn saying. "Artor needs us. Watch over him." Cyn stood and nodded to Riva and they both went back to the trail. Riva noticed that Cyn had a spear as well, he must have found it among the dead bodies.

The rain stopped as they moved away from the battlefield and the sun shone down on them. Riva pulled the hood of her cloak over her head and silently wept as they walked. She would not see those men again and prayed to the gods that she would find her son and manage to avenge their deaths.

After a long walk, the soft ground turned to rock. There was no way of knowing for sure they were on the right trail. Cyn stopped Riva and made her sit on a fallen tree.

He then scouted out ahead to see if he could find another trail. When he came back, he just shook his head.

The sun was low and Cyn started to gather wood for a fire. He pulled out some pyrite and flint, striking it a few times he got a spark big enough to light some dry grass he had kept in his bag. It wasn't long before they had a roaring fire. Riva sat close to Cyn as the fire started to warm them up.

"Tomorrow, we will find them," Cyn said, staring into the fire. When they warmed up a little, Cyn got up and disappeared into the forest. After a few minutes he returned with two small quail. Riva helped him clean and pluck them before putting them over the fire to cook.

After eating Riva put her head on Cyn's shoulder. She was determined not to let herself weep again. Cyn put an arm around her and held her tight. Riva wondered what Artor was doing right now. She hoped he wasn't afraid. He was always a brave child, maybe he was enjoying the adventure. She knew in her heart though, he was likely very scared.

As the sun set, brother and sister sat in their own misery. Cyn felt the loss of Cador, his adoptive father, deeply. Cyn had survived months on his own, his whole family dead when Lirra found him and brought him home. Cador immediately took him in and raised him like his own son.

Riva became his sister, although they didn't look much alike at all. She had light hair and brown eyes, an easy smile and had become a beautiful woman. Cyn swore that she would never be alone, never be unprotected.

They fell asleep as the fire died down. It was a light sleep, filled with bad dreams. By morning they were not well rested. Riva got ready to go quickly. Today they would find Artor!

Chapter 19
Maired

Litana brought news to Maired that there was a guest in the domus. The slaves were talking in the kitchen about the Centurion who had come to visit. She finished feeding Lupinus and got him into clean clothes before getting dressed for the day. She had just finished when there was a knock at the door of the cubiculum.

Litana rushed to answer the door. She turned back to say it was a man named Quintus Tiberius. Maired told her to let the man in. Quintus entered, his presence seemed to fill the room with authority.

"Good morning, domine," Maired said.

"Good morning child," Quintus said. He was looking around the room. Litana had gone to Lupinus' cradle and was bringing him over. His face lit up when he saw the baby.

"Would you like to hold him?" Litana asked.

"Yes!" Quintus said to Maired's surprise. The big man gently took the baby and held him close. Lupinus cooed up at his grandfather. Quintus smiled at the boy.

"He likes you," Litana said.

"He does," Maired said, "as it should be." Quintus looked at Maired with a sad smile.

"I'm sorry that you have been put into this situation Maired," Quintus said. Maired was a little surprised at that statement. He had insisted she come to Rome and live here among strangers.

"Thank you," was all Maired could think to say. She looked around at the small room that had become her whole world. She could get angry with this man, tell him how she felt about being stuck here, but oddly she felt he already understood.

"Come girl," Quintus said to Litana, "come get the child. I must speak with his mother. Give us some privacy." Litana left with the baby and Quintus sat on a stool inviting Maired to recline on the reclinium. Maired joined him, unsure of what he was going to say.

"Do you have news?" Maired asked, concerned, "is Marcus hurt?"

"Nothing like that," Quintus said, "Marcus is well, he has been stationed in Northern Britannia. We are trying to make arrangements for him to come back here for a furlough." Maired smiled, she honestly would be fine if he stayed in Brittania, but she didn't want to let Quintus know.

"That would be nice," Maired said.

"I came to bring you a gift," Quintus said, reaching for a satchel he had carried in. He pulled out a square object wrapped in cloth, "do you read?"

"I can," Maired said. She had taken to reading some of the scrolls that were kept in the house. They were mostly political writings that didn't interest her, but it was something to pass the time.

"Good," Quintus said, unwrapping the package. Inside was a stack of papyrus pages that were stitched together. "This is a copy of the writings of a man named Luke. It tells the story of Iēsus. I would like Lupinus to grow up knowing about Iēsus."

Maired took the papers and looked at them. It would be nice to have something new to read. She looked at the writing, whoever had written it had taken care to make it clear and easy to read.

"Thank you," Maired said sincerely.

"I need to warn you," Quintus said, "there are people in Rome that don't like these writings. Keep them hidden in your room." Maired nodded, it was nice to have a little bit of rebellion in her life.

"Why are you giving it to me?" Maired asked.

"I failed in raising Marcus," Quintus said, "he refuses to listen to anything I tell him about Iēsus. I want to correct that mistake with Lupinus. In our community, I have seen women lead their children to follow Iēsus. I pray you will do the same."

Maired didn't know if she would be able to do what Quintus was asking, but she would read the story and share it with Lupinus. Sharing the stories of your people was incredibly important to Maired, and for Lupinus, Quintus was an ancestor. She knew Iēsus was hated by the Romans, and she hated Romans so maybe it would be good to see what his story was about.

"I will try," Maired said.

"That is all I ask," Quintus said. He stood and called Litana to bring the baby back. "I want to kiss him before I leave." Quintus kissed the top of Lupinus' head before leaving the cubiculum.

Maired watched him go before taking the codex and wrapped it in a piece of cloth before putting it on a shelf. Litana watched her but didn't ask any questions about what she was doing. She just went about her job of caring for Lupinus.

At the end of the day, after Lupinus was in bed, Maired took out the codex and opened it up. Litana was sitting on her mat, mending her own tunic, that was getting threadbare. Maired looked over and felt a little ashamed that she had thought of buying herself a new dress and nothing for this girl.

"What is that?" Litana asked softly.

"A gift from the Centurion," Maired answered. "It is a secret, but he wants me to read it so I can tell Lupinus the stories when he gets older." Litana put down her mending and came closer to Maired.

Maired noticed that the girls under tunic was stained and smelled bad. The Domine of this house should buy her a new one, but the considered Litana to be worthless. She couldn't do many tasks reliably. She often forgot how to do simple tasks for the baby and Maired had to demonstrate again how to do it. Maired decided that the next time she got money, she would buy new clothes for Litana.

"What does it say?" Litana asked.

"If you promise to keep it a secret," Maired said, "we can read it together." Maired opened it up and started reading it aloud. She spoke softly with a strange sense that if someone heard her she might get into trouble, it made her feel alive.

They read the story of the priest who was told his aged wife would have a son by a messenger from a God named Adonai,

Maired had never heard of him. She kept reading that Adonai would give a girl named Miriam a baby, even though she was a virgin. Maired had to explain to Litana that this woman had never been with a man. Litana giggled at the idea, Maired was amused at her innocence.

As they read further, Litana was entranced by the story of the baby sleeping in a manger because there was no room in the house. She mentioned that her sister had slept in an old barrel they had cut in half. Maired shared a smile with her companion.

"Where are you from?" Maired finally asked, unsure why she had not asked before.

"I lived by the sea," Litana said, "I was small when I was sold."

"You were sold?" Maired asked, she had never really Litana about herself.

"My Da sold me," Litana said solemnly, "Ma died having my sister and so he couldn't care for me. I'm too stupid to help." Maired put a hand on Litana's leg, she couldn't believe any man would sell his daughter. She looked over to where Lupinus was sleeping, he may have ruined her life, but she couldn't sell him into slavery.

"You help me," Maired said. Litana smiled so big her nose crinkled up.

"I'm glad I was brought to you," Litana said, "Lupinus is a good baby. I just love him." Maired smiled, she was glad someone could love him. Litana yawned and Maired closed the codex.

"It's late," you should sleep. Litana nodded obediently and went over to her own mat. As she got under her small wool blanket she sighed.

"Can we read more tomorrow?" Litana asked.

"Yes," Maired said. "Just remember, we don't tell anyone." Litana let out a loud yawn and was snoring before Maired could get the small stack of papers wrapped up and back on the shelf.

Chapter 20
Taran

A group of guests were sitting at one of the tables, drinking ale and exchanging stories of their travels. Taran stood in the kitchen and listened to them. He longed to be sitting with them, telling his own stories, but that wasn't his place anymore. Samira put her hand on his forearm and when he looked at her, she smiled.

"You will travel again," Samira said gently.

"I know," Taran said. "Even if I don't, I have you and Nura." He kissed Samira before going back into the tabiculum, the little office off the kitchen. He needed to make sure he had a good record of the charges for the day. As he wrote all the figures on a wax tablet, he considered the future. His mother was a good hostess; she wasn't good with money. He would stay here until he knew someone could help her. His cousin Llyr, Seren's oldest, was good with figures, but he worked with his father all the time.

Taran put down his stylus, he would find a solution later. The guests had all gone to their cubiculae by the time Taran was done with the record keeping. Some men were coming through the arch, and Taran saw his mother greeting them.

Taran knew these were the Christians who met with his mother on a regular basis. They always came under the cover of darkness and would head up to the family quarters to discuss the teachings of their God. Maeli had explained that there were some people that didn't like what they were doing and everything had to be done secretly.

Gaius usually led the discussions; Taran would sit in when he could. His mother had accepted the teaching of Iēsus fully, but Taran still he questions. Gaius said that Iēsus had been crucified, Taran had seen many crucifixions in his travels. Criminals would be hung from a cross on major roads to remind people of the power of Rome. Apparently Iēsus had not committed any crime, which was likely, the Romans tended to be quick to kill anyone they suspected of being a criminal. What made no sense to Taran was the claim that Iēsus had come back to life. He had never known anyone to come back to life.

Taran would stay in the kitchen for tonight's meetings. He normally did when they had a full inn. It was important to know that nobody was spying on them. Samira sat with him and she gave Nura to Taran. He held his little girl in his arms and looked into her light eyes. For a moment he wondered about Maired, she would have had her baby by now. He wondered if it was a boy or a girl.

"We should send a message to Maired," Taran said.

"One of the guests is from Rome," Samira said, "he might be able to get a message to her." Taran walked to the tabiculum to get his ink, reed pen and papyrus. Samira took Nura back so he could use his knife to sharpen the reed. Once it had a good point, Taran dipped it into the ink and started a message.

After writing a greeting, Taran wasn't sure what to write. Samira suggested he start with the good news about Nura. The two crafted a message that gave the news from the past year. Once they had written it, Taran folded the papyrus and tied it with a cord. He melted some wax to seal the knot in the cord and keep the letter sealed. Taran placed the letter on the table in the tabiculum.

The meeting upstairs had ended and people were leaving the caupona. Taran locked the gate as Samira went up the stairs. As he walked back across the courtyard he ran into a guest in the courtyard. It was a trader, a Roman man who specialized in trading linens and wool.

"Is there anything you need?" Taran asked.

"Who were those people?" the guest asked.

"Friends of my mother," Taran said honestly.

"They are here late," the guest observed. Taran tried to decide if the man was suspicious or just nosey.

"They all work hard during the day," Taran said, "then gossip until late in the evening." Taran tried to make it sound as innocent as he could. The guest smiled and nodded.

"My mother would do that as well," the guest said, laughing as he went to his cubiculum. Taran shook his head and then rushed up the stairs. They were getting everything cleaned up from the meeting when he arrived. He thought about telling everyone about the nosey guest but thought better of it. There was no cause to worry them.

Taran lay in bed thinking about the letter they had written to Maired. The linen trader was the man he was planning to ask to deliver his letter. Now he wondered if that was a good idea. He tried to remember if he mentioned Gaius or the meetings in the letter. The letter was sealed, but he didn't have an impression to prove he had sealed it. Anyone could read it and then reseal it.

He decided not to send the letter until he had rewritten it. That would also give his mother the opportunity to add something to it. This gave him peace of mind and he went to sleep. He had bad dreams all night of the Romans coming and arresting his mother. When he woke up the next morning, he was not well rested.

As he settled with some of the guests, he found himself face to face with the linen merchant. He wanted to make sure the man wasn't suspicious of the meeting but then realized asking about his suspicions was suspicious.

"I hope your time in Brittania was profitable," Taran said to the merchant.

"It was," the man replied. That didn't give Taran much information, but he didn't dare pry. They bartered the final ratio for the stay and the man paid before leaving.

"Did you give him the letter?" Samira asked as she joined him.

"I decided to wait," Taran said, "give Ma a chance to add something."

"That's a good idea," Samira said. She kissed his cheek and walked off to the kitchen. She used a linen cloth to carry Nura, the baby, keeping her pressed against Samira's chest. The cloth wrapped tightly around them and supporting her head and body securely. Samira went to work on her tasks in the kitchen. Taran was impressed that she could still do all her work and care for the baby.

Taran went to the tablinum to count out the coins and lock them safely away. He saw the letter on the table and put it into the lock box as well. He had kept out a share of the coins for Eòin and Teleri. He found Teleri cleaning a cubiculum and handed her a share.

"Thank you," Teleri said. "Did you hear the news?" Taran thought for a moment, he couldn't think of any news.

"I've been betrothed to Ceredig the younger," Teleri said beaming. Taran smiled, Ceredig the younger came from a farming family. He didn't know the boy well, but he knew he was a hard worker. He had long black hair and a gently curving jawline that would likely get more square as he aged. He also seemed to be grinning or laughing every time Taran saw him.

"He's a good match for you," Taran said, which made Teleri's smile seem to get bigger.

"He is," Teleri said. "I'll bring him by soon, his Da is hoping he can work here." That made sense. Taran knew a lot of marriage betrothals were made because a father thought it would help their child establish a strong future. Teleri went back to work while Taran searched for Eòin.

Taran thought about having someone else working here. If he could trust Ceredig to deal with the money, he might be able to travel again.

Chapter 21
Riva

Cyn shook Riva awake. As her brown eyes fluttered open she saw him smiling down at her. The sun was already well above the horizon; it was getting late. Cyn was pointing to the East.

"I found the village," Cyn said. Riva sat up to put on her shoes. She tied the leather wraps around her feet and got up.

"How far?" Riva asked excitedly.

"Close," Cyn said. Riva followed her brother through the forest. She realized he was avoiding all trails where people might see them. They came to a small clump of roundhouses with a tall stone broch jutting out above them. The broch was the tower where the women and children would go in time of attack. There were people moving around the small village, going about their daily routine.

The people didn't look like murderous villains, but like normal people. Riva would have preferred them to look evil. She spotted the man that had broken into her roundhouse. He was laughing and talking to a young girl. She looked frightened, he used the bottom end of his spear to raise her skirt and expose the bottom of her legs. Riva felt some odd satisfaction in seeing him treat a woman that way. She was going to kill him, it was nice to know she would be doing the world a favor. The girl rushed away, and then Riva spotted Artor.

He was standing behind the man who had taken him. He was holding on to the man's leg, looking around at the people. Riva could see the fear in his eyes. She could feel the rush of warm blood coming to her face. She was ready to kill the man now.

Cyn placed a hand on her arm, and nodded as if he could read her mind. Growing up he had often sensed what she was thinking, it was her one consolation that he was still here. Cyn pointed to a small clump of bushes closer to the village, on the edge of the tree line. Riva followed him to the bushes.

Cyn climbed into the bushes and smoothed out an area for himself and Riva to sit. He then beckoned her quietly to join him. She sat down, she wished she was as good at reading his mind as he was hers.

"Now we watch," Cyn whispered. "We wait." Riva didn't like that plan, but she understood it. To attack in the daylight was foolish. So, they would watch and wait.

It was torturous to watch the big man dragging her son around. As the sun rose higher, she could see that Artor was getting tired. He often would sleep for a while during the day. Artor was lagging and the evil man dragged him over to a roundhouse close to the broch. A woman came out of the house and the man said something to her. She gently took Artor into the house.

Riva could see from the expression on Cyn's face that he was thinking of a plan. The man's roundhouse was far from the tree line. If they decided to rescue Artor at night, they would have to cross a lot of space before reaching the house or returning. She tried to think of a plan, but it wasn't something she was used to doing.

"We can get him back when they sleep," Riva whispered to Cyn. Cyn nodded, he must have been thinking the same.

"We will start there," Cyn pointed to a spot where a roundhouse was built close to the tree line. "We should rest now." Cyn carefully got up and then helped Riva out of the bush. He led her to a small hollow at the base of a tree, big enough for one person to lay in. Cyn indicated that she should rest first and he would keep watch.

Riva curled up in the hollow. The moss that was growing across the wood and ground was soft and she managed to close her eyes and get some rest. She had slept well the night before, but knew she needed all her strength for tonight. When Cyn shook her awake, they traded places so he could rest. His eyes were swollen from lack of sleep.

Riva sat on a tree root and kept watch. She had Eiran's spear by her side. She thought back to the day Artor was born. Eiran was in awe of the little person that they had made. Anytime Artor cried or fussed Eiran would be concerned. He never told people how he felt, but he showed it with his attention. That was how Riva had known he had loved her; he always did what he could to care for her.

The sun was starting to set, and Riva quietly went back to the bush. She saw Artor playing in the dirt outside of that same roundhouse. After a while the woman called him in, he was such a good child he obeyed the stranger. She stayed until the sun came down, then went back to Cyn to wake him.

They waited as the air grew colder. The moon was hidden by heavy clouds, giving little light, which would make their task a little easier. Cyn led the way to where they could sneak into the village, he pulled out his knife and gave it to Riva before crossing the threshold of the tree line into the open.

They crossed the small open area, Riva expected to hear a cry of alarm with every step, but the village was silent. They moved around the roundhouses keeping to the darkest shadows until they found the one Artor was in. Riva prayed to the gods that the door wouldn't be locked, they had a beam in their home that could be placed across the door to secure it. On a night like this, with everything secure, it shouldn't be locked.

Cyn gently pushed the door open, and they quietly inched around it. Opening it fully would let a blast of cold air in and could wake the people inside. In the soft glow from the embers, they could see a table and stools to their right. Beyond that was a bed where the evil man was laying with his woman. They were asleep. Across the hearth from them she spotted the small blonde head of Artor peeking out from under a woolen blanket.

She pointed the boy out to Cyn and stepped to one side to let Cyn go to Artor. He would try to carry him out without waking him. Riva moved softly to where the evil man was sleeping. She glared at him; pure hatred filled her. As Cyn picked up Artor, a part of the bed shifted, making a loud noise. The eyes of the evil man fluttered open, and then Riva saw surprise on his face as he saw her standing over him.

Without a moment's hesitation Riva took the knife slit the man's throat. She felt an instant gratification as his warm blood started to spurt out and covered her hands. The woman woke up and saw what was happening and jumped up. The woman saw Cyn holding Artor and rushed to him, picking up a burning stick from the fire. She swung the stick just missing Artor. Riva picked up her spear and thrust it into the woman, feeling her flesh give way to the sharp point quickly.

Riva pulled the spear back and the woman fell to the ground. Cyn didn't hesitate for a moment but threw the door open and ran out of the roundhouse as fast as he could. Artor woke up as they hit the cold air. He was about to yell and Cyn shushed him. Recognizing the voice of one of his favorite people, Artor buried his head into Cyn's shoulder as they made their way to the forest. Without warning the skies opened and dumped rain on them.

Once in the woods, Cyn handed Artor to Riva. The boy cried when he saw his mother. Riva carried him through the forest, the rain and the trees dampening the noise. The people of the village likely wouldn't know anything was wrong until the morning. Cyn led them around large boulders and through creeks formed by the downpour. Riva had no idea how he could know where he was going but trusted him.

The sun was touching the horizon as they came to a trail. The rain had slowed down but was still coming down. Artor had fallen asleep in Riva's arms. Cyn had offered to carry him, but Riva didn't want to let him go. As daylight approached, they came to the cave opening. Cyn led them inside where it was dry.

Riva removed Artor's wet clothes and wrapped him in a blanket and he immediately fell into a deep sleep. Cyn got the fire going and came back to Riva. She looked down at her dress; she was covered in the man's blood. The rain had diluted it, but she could still see where it had sprayed her. She took it off and sat on a rock in her damp under tunic.

Cyn quietly picked it up and disappeared out of the cave. Riva moved closer to the fire and sat looking at the flames. She had done it, she had rescued her son and avenged her husband. Cyn came back in, wearing only his under tunic. He hung her dress and his own tunic on the cave wall, she noticed he had managed to get more of the blood out. He sat next to her by the fire and stared into the flames. He then poked her with his elbow and they both laughed.

Chapter 22
Maired

The reading of the codex had become a nightly ritual for Maired and Litana. Sometimes they would lay Lupinus on the bed and Litana would play with him while they read, other times they would wait until he was asleep. They had even made up a code phrase for the activity; they called it story time. If Litana accidentally mentioned it in the city, or somewhere people could hear it seemed ordinary. Gauls and Britons were both storytelling people.

There were some stories that Maired felt had to be exaggerated. There was no way they were able to feed five thousand men with five loaves of bread and two fish. Litana thought maybe they just each ate a little bit. Most evenings they ended up talking and even laughing about the stories.

Litana had asked questions about the devil that tried to get Iēsus to go against his father Adonai. Maired wasn't sure how to answer. She didn't know of any of these gods or their stories. She started to keep notes of questions to ask Quintus if she saw him again. She wished there were more people to talk to about these stories. They were all interesting.

Since they were almost at the end, Litana asked if they could start early this evening to read it all the way to the end. Maired agreed and they sat up on the bed with some food, the baby and the codex. As was their habit, they had put a stool in front of the door so nobody could come in.

Maired started reading about Iēsus and his followers having a meal. The story called it the Seder mean. Litana asked about Seder and Maired wrote that down on her list.

"When we have all the answers to these questions," Maired said as she wrote the words down, "we will have to read it again. Maybe things will make more sense."

"I don't need to understand it all to know one thing," Litana said, "I like Iēsus. He's kind to the children." Maired nodded, she agreed with that part. They had both enjoyed the story where Iēsus scolded the men that were keeping the women and children away from him. Maired agreed that she wished she could meet someone as wise and kind as Iēsus.

They kept reading about the meal and Iēsus mentioned that someone would betray him. Litana sat still, her eyes large when the guard came to arrest Iēsus in the story. When Iēsus put the ear back on the man after his follower cut it off Litana shook her head.

"He's so nice," Litana said softly. "Why are they arresting him?"

"They don't like what he said about their gods," Maired said. She wasn't totally sure, but it was why she had to hide the codex from others. She continued reading about the trial and it made more sense. They said he told people not to pay taxes to Caesar. Maired knew that was a serious offense and people would be sold into slavery to pay for their taxes.

"He didn't say any of that," Litana said loudly. Maired hushed her and shook her head, smiling. Litana had a strong sense of justice, reading these lies were making her angry. "Remember he said to give Caesar things that are his," Litana said softly.

"You're right!" Maired said, "they had to lie because he didn't do anything against Rome." Maired had heard about this happening, people lying to Roman magistrates to get other people arrested. Roman magistrates don't care what you do so long as you don't break their laws. She kept reading.

The room became tense as they read anoint Iēsus being beaten and then crucified. Maired had seen her first crucifixion when she was ten years old. She had been with her father, going to Londinium when they passed ten men nailed to wooded structures on the roadside. They were still alive, but every breath was torture for them. She had asked her father a thousand questions about what was going on. He had explained they were criminals who had been sentenced to die. It wasn't until she thought about it later did, she realize it was the first time she had seen a man naked, in the moment she didn't even realize what she was looking at.

Litana was weeping quietly as Maired read about Iēsus dying. Maired had a hard time keeping her voice strong. When she read about him being buried in another man's tomb she started to weep as well. Maired stopped reading. Litana sniffed and turned to look at Lupinus, who was staring at them and cooing.

"I thought you couldn't kill a god!" Litana said softly through her tears. Maired shook her head and looked back through the codex. How could anyone still be telling the story of a god who could be killed by Rome. What was the good of Iēsus if he was dead? Why did Quintus want Lupinus to know all of this?

"There are a few pages left," Maired said, "let's read on and see what happens." Litana shook her head and sniffed. Lupinus let out a little giggle. Both women turned to him and Litana let out a small laugh.

Maired started back reading the story, she felt sorry for the women that had wanted to prepare Iēsus but could not because of some law called Shabbat. She understood from the context of the story that Shabbat meant you weren't supposed to work. Then they finally arrived and found the tomb empty.

"Why is it empty?" Litana asked. "Who moved it?" Maired shrugged, she wasn't sure of anything in this strange tale. She just kept reading about the two men who shone like the sun telling them that Iēsus had come back from the dead.

"Of course!" Litana said victoriously, "He raised other people from the dead. Of course he is the god of life! You think he can be killed, but he can't!" Maired wasn't sure that was true, but it did make sense.

"That makes sense," Maired said. Litana looked so happy that she had figured something out for herself. They finished the codex and after they read about Iēsus ascending into the sky they sat and stared at the pages, each lost in their own thoughts.

Maired wondered if Iēsus was in the otherworld or if there was another place he might be. He talked of the Kingdom of Adonai, maybe that was different. Maired made a note to ask Quintus. She wrapped up the codex and her notes in a cloth and put them away.

"Can we start over again tomorrow?" Litana asked.

"Why?" Maired asked.

"I enjoy our story time." Litana responded.

Chapter 23
Marcus

Marcus lifted the flap of his tent and stepped into daylight. He had strapped on his breastplate and caligae in the tent. He put his helmet on outside since he was expected to wear it while on guard. It was uncomfortable and he hated wearing it. He took his shield and pilum, a short spear, from their place by the tent.

Marcus was part of the century assigned to a large trading party in Caledonia. It was a boring assignment; the only redeeming thing was that one of the traders had an attractive slave. He could see the tent where the slaves slept from his post on guard and would watch her coming and going, imagining being with her.

He walked to his post; this was their last night before packing up and leaving for Londinium. Marcus took his post as the sun was moving lower in the sky. He took his post and stood watching both the road and the slaves' quarters. Marcus hated how quickly this country went from daytime to darkness, before long he was in the dark unable to see anything but the glow of lanterns in the camp.

Marcus loved the power of being a part of the most powerful military force in the world. He was a low-ranking man in the fort, but in the streets, he was an enforcer of the power of Rome! People had to listen to him. His training had made him stronger than he was before, and he felt he could take on any enemy.

As the camp went to sleep, Marcus wrapped his cape around his shoulders. He couldn't wait to get back to the warmth of Rome, even if that meant spending time with Maired. He had resented being forced to marry her, she was nothing to him. He had been fascinated by her red hair, but he didn't want to spend his life with her. Her one redeeming quality was that she had given him a son.

There was a rustle of leaves outside the camp. Marcus imagined it was only the wind but had been told enough times that if he missed an enemy because he wasn't cautious, he would be punished. He had been forced to stand for hours in the hot sun holding a heavy pack for being late once. Missing an enemy attack would mean a worse punishment. Marcus turned to the legionary, Flavius, who was posted with him.

"Did you hear something?" Marcus asked quietly. Flavius nodded. "I'm going to see if there is anything out there," Marcus said. He handed his pilum to Flavius and moved swiftly towards a clump of trees. He was certain this was the source of the sound.

The trees were dark against the night sky, standing like the columns of the forum. Marcus moved as quietly as he could with the armor on. There were some shadows ahead that were moving. Marcus got a little closer and realized they were men. Without another thought, Marcus turned and rushed back to the camp.

"Raiders!" Marcus yelled as he ran to the camp, "raise the alarm!" Flavius planted Marcus' pilum in the soil and rushed to wake the camp. Marcus grabbed his pilum and shield and stood ready. The raiders, recognizing they had been seen, gave out a blood curdling battle cry and started to rush the camp.

The highly trained century of legionaries came to life faster than the raiders could have imagined. Marcus could feel his comrades joining him to stand in line to face the raiders. They used their shields to form a wall, which made it difficult to see the raiders, but would make it impossible for the raiders to break through.

It wasn't long before the raiders hit the wall, slashing with swords and axes to break through. The shouted command came down the line, and the legion shifted their shields and thrust their pilum. Marcus didn't hit anything, but it didn't matter. What mattered was working in unison.

Another order came and the legion stepped forward, pushing against the raiders. There was some resistance, but the raiders were pushed back. They had to step over the bodies of dead or dying raiders. With another thrust with the pilum and another step forward, the legion advanced in unison. Each man doing exactly what they were trained to do.

Only once did Marcus feel the weight of an axe hitting his shield. When he thrust his pilum through it didn't connect with anyone, which was a disappointment to him. It wasn't long before the raiders were pushed back to the trees, and they disappeared into the trees, retreating in defeat. The legionaries did not cheer or celebrate; they just returned to their posts.

"Well done men," was all they received as a reward from the Centurion. They had done as expected. Marcus finished his watch and then went to get some sleep. The next morning, he would be expected to march with the century back towards the fort. Once they got to the fort, they would be relieved.

Two days later they walked through the gates of the fort. Marcus felt a sense of relief. He would still have watch duties, but it would be in guard towers that had shelter from the cold and rain. He could sleep in his comfortable bed in the barracks again and not in a crowded tent. Most importantly there were beautiful women in the fort and surrounding town.

When Marcus entered the barracks, he saw an old friend. Claudius Maximus had been with his father's century when he was working as a calō. He had often joined the group that came to the Caupona Caureni.

"Marcus!" Claudius exclaimed as he came in, "good to see you!"

"Good to see you," Marcus said, "how have you been?"

"Good," Claudius said, "I've been assigned here while Centurion Quintus is in Rome."

"My father's in Rome?" Marcus asked. Since becoming a legionary, Marcus had not seen much of his father. That suited him, he could make his own way without any help from the old man.

"Yes," Claudius said, "he's taken some important information from the governor of Brittania." Claudius lowered his voice, "and he's doing some work for the master." Marcus had to think for a moment and then realized what he meant by that. Marcus hated that his father had rejected the Roman gods. They used code words when talking like "the master" or "the teacher," Marcus had tried hard to forget that his father was a traitor to Ceasar.

"I see," Marcus said. He walked away to put his weapons on the rack in the barrack. He wished he could stop his father from worshipping a different God but wasn't sure what he could do. The meetings that he helped set up were an excuse to get together to discuss the God Iēsus. Marcus had a realization, if he could stop the meetings, maybe then his father would give up on the foolishness. He found Claudius and pulled him aside.

"Do you know if the meetings are still going on?" Marcus asked.

"A few people meet," Claudius said. "At least when I was there a few months ago." Marcus thanked Claudius and rushed to his Centurion's quarters. His Centurion was a smallish man, about the same height as Marcus, but not as broad. He was very intelligent and always was thinking of his men and how to make them more efficient. He was out of his armor and stood there in his red tunic. His short cropped black hair was slicked back with oil.

"Domine Centurion," Marcus said, "I have received word of a Christian meeting in the region." The Centurion showed Marcus in, he had often spoken against the Christians, he was loyal to Caesar and nobody else.

"Meeting is not illegal," the Centurion said cautiously.

"They are meeting in a caupona," Marcus said. He knew that they could cause a problem for a group meeting in a public place. The Centurions face lit up.

"Tell me more," the Centurion said.

Chapter 24
Riva

Artor was enjoying spending time with Cyn in the cave. He had asked for his Da a time or two, but this adventure was enough of a distraction for him. Riva was happy that her son liked it here, but she couldn't build a home here. It was good for Cyn, but not big enough for the family.

"I will need to find a new home," Riva said to Cyn one evening by the fire. Cyn nodded solemnly. It had been nice having them here, but he also enjoyed his privacy.

"Da and Ma moved when we were younger," Cyn said. Riva had often heard the story of them moving to get away from her mother's abusive father. Riva's father had beaten the man and then they moved. It had been hard, but they had each other, and their slave Riona. Riva loved Riona and was glad her father had given her freedom. She had met a man and wanted to marry and he let her.

Riva knew she could find a new home, but how was she supposed do it? She didn't have a man, She didn't have any family to help her get settled. Cyn might be willing, but he hated being around people.

"What should I do?" Riva whispered.

"Taran," Cyn said softly. They had
met Taran years ago, when he was passing
through the area. She knew nothing about
him, other than the fact he ran a caupona in
Briton, under Roman control. Riva had been
raised to hate the Romans, but she needed
family help.

"You're right," Riva said, "maybe he
can help."

The next morning Riva packed some
food and what little they had for the journey.
Cyn would lead her to the boundary of
Roman control, and she would be on her own
from there. It would take her a little over two
weeks to get to Caerwyn if everything went
well.

The journey to the frontier went
quickly, and Cyn showed Riva a few things
she didn't know about finding food in the
wilderness. It wasn't long before Riva was an
expert at setting snares and catching small
animals for meat. With her knowledge of what
plants she could eat she would be able to keep
herself and Artor alive until they got to the
caupona.

On the day Cyn kissed her cheek and
hugged both her and Artor goodbye, Riva felt
the most despair she had in a while. She felt
like this would be the last time she saw her
brother. She held his head so she looked in

his eyes and told him she loved him and would never forget what he did for her and Artor. He never said that he loved her, he didn't need to. He turned back and walked away without looking back.

Riva and Artor crossed the frontier quickly and moved through the woods to a Roman road. They would look like a normal mother and son walking down the road and shouldn't attract any attention. In the evening, Riva found a place in the woods for them to camp.

This became their daily routine, walking as long as they could and then camp in the forest. Artor asked to be carried some of the time but mostly walked on his own. They made slow progress, but they did keep moving ahead.

One day a group of Roman legionaries was walking down the road. Artor had never seen legionaries before and was in awe. Riva understood, for a boy the big men in shiny armor and spears must be an amazing sight. For Riva it meant oppression.

The further south they travelled the more Roman influence Riva saw. The big villas and cauponae on the side of the road were amazing to look at. Riva wondered how people could live with all that space in their homes. It seemed like a lot of work to maintain.

Finally, Riva saw the sign her father had talked about. The triskelion carved into a wooden sign hanging by a arched entrance to the building. Riva took a deep breath and took Artor's hand. She walked through the arch and saw an open space with a well in the middle. To her right were four doors and to her left an open kitchen. There was a small opening in the wall across from her.

Walking through the opening was the man she recognized as Taran. He saw her and smiled as he walked over. Riva wondered if he recognized her, it had been a while since they had seen each other.

"Are you looking for a room?" Taran asked helpfully. He hadn't remembered her.

"Not really," Riva said, "I'm looking for you."

"Me?" Taran asked, seeming a little taken aback. Then realization crossed his face as he recognized her. "Riva?" he asked, "it's amazing to see you. What are you doing here?"

"It's a long story," Riva said.

"Come," Taran said, "sit down." Taran led Riva over to the kitchen where a woman with a darker complexion was preparing a meal. "Samira!" Taran said, "this is Riva, my Caledonian relative." The woman came over to greet Riva. She had such beautiful dark hair, and dark brown eyes, then Riva noticed the child tied to her chest.

"Riva," the woman said, "what a nice name. Who is this?" the woman indicated Artor.

"My son Artor," Riva said. Samira indicated a chair to Riva who sat gratefully. Artor was not interested in sitting and was wandering around the kitchen. Samira took his hand.

"Artor," Samira said gently, "do you like horses?" Artor shook his head, his eyes huge. "Let's go look at the horses and your Ma can talk to Taran." Samira led Artor to the opening in the wall facing the arch.

"They'll be fine," Taran said, "Ceredig is in there, he'll watch the boy." Riva nodded her head gently. She had not realized how tired she was until she sat. She tried to control her emotions but started to weep. Taran sat next to her and put his arm around her shoulder. He didn't say anything, just sat and held her. She knew she would be safe with him.

A woman came down the steps and saw them. She had white hair and a stern looking face.

"What's wrong?" the lady asked.

"This is Riva," Taran said, "Cador's daughter." The woman immediately sat with her and took over comforting Riva. Taran stood and beckoned a young girl with blonde hair, a little darker than Riva's. The girl rushed over to help. "Go get your Ma, Cador's daughter is here," Taran said to the girl. She rushed off as quickly as she could.

Taran sat again, across from Riva. Samira came out of the stable, Artor was following holding the hands of a young man with straight black hair. Both were smiling and laughing. It made Riva feel like things would be alright. She took a deep breath.

"I'm sorry," Riva said, "it's been a long journey."

"That is a long journey," Taran said. "Longer with such a small child." Riva smiled at her son who was now running in circles around the well with the boy chasing him.

"He's a good boy," Riva said, "never complained." Riva sniffed and accepted a tankard of ale from Samira. The drink calmed her down some more. "My father and husband are dead," she said suddenly. The woman with white hair gasped,

"Your Da visited me when my husband passed, he was a good man." Riva realized this must be Maeli. Her father had told her about the redheaded girl his brother had married. Her hair had gone completely white, but she still looked young.

"So, you came here for help?" Taran asked.

"I have no other family," Riva said. Taran nodded his head. "I need some time to decide what to do next."

"Of course you do," Maeli said, "and we can use your help as well." Riva tilted her head, she never thought about them needing her help. She felt a little better realizing that she was not the only one who needed help.

"What do you need my help with?" Riva asked.

"We have this Caupona to run," Maeli said, "it's a big job." Riva thought back to stories her father had told her about this caupona. Her father's father had earned it by saving the life of a wealthy Roman. How her father had run the stables and cared for the animals. Romans came to rely on this caupona for travel and trade.

"Are you certain I will be helpful?" Riva asked. "I don't know anything about it."

"This old place is in our blood," Taran answered. "It's our history, our land." Riva was certain they had forgotten the old ways. That they had forgotten that the land was soaked in the blood of the ancestors and became a part of them. She gave a small smile and looked around at her family.

"I have no place else," Riva said, "and I will do everything in my power to help." Another woman, this one with blonde hair and blue eyes rushed into the kitchen. She looked at Riva and let out a small gasp.

"You have your father's eyes," the woman said.

"This is Cador's sister," Maeli said.

"Seren?" Riva asked, looking up at her father's closest remaining family member.

"Riva," Seren said, "it is nice to finally meet you." Seren sat and listened to Riva's news that Cador was dead. She had tears in her eyes but did not weep. She knew at their last meeting she would likely not see him again.

They spent the afternoon together, Riva telling them about her husband and brother Cyn. Taran and Samira stepped away from time to time to tend to the business of the caupona, but Maeli and Seren were very attentive.

Seren told stories of her brother, how he was not the most sociable person. She listened to Riva tell stories about him defending his wife from her father. She shook her head, that was Cador. Loyal to the ones he loved. As the sun started to set Artor climbed onto his mother's lap and fell asleep.

"You two need a place to sleep," Maeli said.

"We have an empty cubiculum tonight," Taran said, "we will find a long-term home tomorrow." Taran led Riva to one of the doors opposite the kitchen. Riva was shocked when they went inside. There was a big bed, with a padded mattress and several cushions. There was a table, stools and another small bed with a curved end. Taran said it was for reclining instead of sitting.

Riva put Artor in the big bed as Taran lit a small oil lamp. He wished her good night and left her alone. Riva wanted to weep again. Everything here was different. As she undressed for bed, she wondered how people slept in a room with no fire. When she got into the bed it made more sense, there were two wool blankets for warmth. As she lay down, Artor snuggled in close, at least that felt like home.

Chapter 25
Litana

Litana rushed to the door to quiet whoever was knocking. Domina Maired was still sleeping, and she didn't want to wake her. When she opened the door, the old Centurion was standing there. He had just been there the day before and stayed late. That was why Domina Maired was tired.

"Is your Domina here?" the Centurion asked.

"Yes Domine," Litana said, "she is sleeping."

"Of course," the Centurion replied, "I kept her up late." He had not planned to stay so long the day before, but these two young women had so many questions. He answered as many as he could and took their list to ask others. It had been one of his happiest moments in a long time. Quintus pulled out a folded parchment, sealed with his insignia and handed it to Litana.

"Don't wake her," Quintus said, "just give her this." Litana took the parchment and thanked Quintus. He left and she closed the door as softly as possible. Maired was sleeping and Lupinus was waving his arms in his cradle. He often entertained himself for a little while in the morning. If he was dry and well fed he was happy.

Litana put the parchment on the table and quietly left to get the food for the day. She had to go down the slave's corridor to get to the kitchen. It was a long way, and she had to remember to turn at the second to last entrance. The last one was the bath, she didn't like the bath, it was hot and smelly. The kitchen was hot and smelly too, but a good smelly. Litana laughed at herself for thinking that, it was funny, the kitchen was a good smelly.

When she arrived the head cook, a big woman who always wore her grey hair in a knot on her head and had red cheeks greeted her. The woman pointed to a tray of food for Maired. As Litana picked up the tray a small clay jar of wine fell and broke on the floor.

"Watch it!" the cook said, hitting Litana behind her left ear. Her ear started to ring but she ignored that and tried to clean up the mess.

"Sorry," Litana said, she almost called the cook "Domina," but knew that would get her a lashing. Only the Domina and Domina Maired could be called that.

"Leave that you fool," the cook said, "I will clean it." The cook picked up another

jar of wine from a shelf and handed it to
Litana.

"Thank you," Litana said as she
quickly carried the tray out. She walked back
down the corridor carefully. She remembered
to put the tray on the floor before opening
the door. Then she carried it in. Maired was
waking up and Litana quickly put the tray on
the table and rushed to help Maired.

After Maired had dressed and was
feeding the baby, Litana remembered the
parchment the Centurion had given her. She
had been thinking about it, hoping it had
more answers about their story time. She took
it to Maired and explained what it was. Maired
opened it and read it quietly.

"Litana," Maired said after reading it,
"we need to get ready to head to town."
Litana nodded her head. She would change
the baby and then put on the new tunic that
Maired had bought her. She liked it and the
under tunic, both were soft.

They went into the big noisy city
again. Litana hated the city, it was easy to get
lost. She had been lost a few times when sent
out on her own. Fortunately, the Domina of
her house finally stopped sending her out. She
had been so happy when Domina Maired
came, and she was told to take care of Maired
and the baby.

Lupinus was such a handsome baby, she loved him immediately. Domina Maired was always so sad, Litana loved her too. The story time had made Domina Maired happy, which is part of why she wanted to keep story time going. Litana also enjoyed listening to what Iēsus said. She wondered if Iēsus could make her brain work better.

Maired led them down a small alleyway and through a small doorway. She talked to a lady who was standing just inside and then turned back and walked in a different direction. Litana realized that she was lost. Then she saw the old Centurion ahead, she pointed him out to Domina Maired who smiled and rushed to meet him.

"Welcome Maired," Quintus said, "I'm glad you found it."

"It wasn't easy," Maired said with a smile.

"Good, I want it that way," Quintus said, "I have a surprise for you." Quintus led them through a small door into a long corridor. There were doors coming off the corridor, evenly spaced. Quintus took her to the end of the corridor and up a flight of stairs to an identical corridor heading back across the building. They went to the third door and Quintus opened it.

The door let into a simple room, it had a table with two reclinia and two beds. There were shelves on one wall and the other three were bare. The plaster was crumbling in a few areas and walls were yellowing with age. There was a window on the far wall that let in little light. Quintus looked around, smiling.

"Welcome home," Quintus said.

"I don't understand," Maired said.

"This insulae is owned by a widow," Quintus said, "who is a follower of the way." Quintus had explained to Maired the day before that Iēsus called himself "the way" so his followers used that term instead of Christians. They didn't like to advertise their beliefs since Ceasar Domitian hated them and tried to stop them from telling others their beliefs. "She is letting you live here."

"I still don't understand," Maired said slowly.

"After our conversation yesterday," Quintus said reclining and indicating that Maired should as well. "I realized you want to follow Iēsus." Maired nodded, he was right, she liked the answers Quintus had for her questions, things made more sense now. Litana wanted to tell them she wanted to follow Iēsus as well, but it wasn't her place to speak.

"I think I do," Maired said.

"This insulae is filled with other followers," Quintus said softly, "they help each other however they can. Prisca is the widow that organizes everything. She will be here soon."

"How will I eat?" Maired asked, "I got my food free."

"The group all pools their money," Quintus said, "I have already told them to send your allowance here. Litana was happy that Domina Maired would be able to live here. Maybe she would find people she could be friends with. People who were smart like she was.

"What about Litana?" Maired asked. Litana was surprised that her Domina had thought of her.

"That was easier than I thought it would be," Quintus said. "When I mentioned to my relatives that I was moving you out they insisted you take that fool girl with you." Quintus turned to Litana, "I'm sorry, that's what they said."

"They always call me that," Litana said.

"She is not the fool everyone thinks she is," Maired said, "she understood more about what Iēsus taught than I did;" Maired smiled, "at least at first." Litana had never had such a nice thing said about her. She didn't know what to do so she looked down at the baby in her arms. Lupinus was smiling up at her and making baby noises that didn't mean anything.

There was a light knock on the door and a woman walked in. She had grey hair and a heavily lined face. Litana immediately liked her, she looked so kind.

"This is Prisca," Quintus said. Maired stood to greet her. Prisca gave her a hug and then held her at arm's length to look at her.

"Your hair is like a flame," Prisca said, "amazing!"

"Thank you," Maired said softly. Prisca went to Litana and the baby and moved the blanket that was covering his face a little.

"A blessing from Adonai," Prisca said, "what is his name?"

"Lupinus," Maired said.

"The little wolf," Prisca said, she looked at Litana with a smile, "and who are you, little one?"

"I'm Litana," Litana said, "I am Domina Maired's slave." Prisca shook her head.

"We are not gentile or Jew, slave nor free, male or female, all are the same in our Lord Iēsus," Prisca said, "Paulos wrote that, and I believe it." Litana wasn't sure who Paulos was, but she wanted to believe it too.

"My mother has a letter from Paulos!" Maired said.

"Is she a follower?" Prisca asked.

"I'm not sure," Maired said. Quintus frowned and stood to join the ladies.

"She is," Quintus said, "I'm going to visit her soon, but she's joined meetings and understands the way."

"I was always more interested in Marcus. I should have come to the meetings instead." Maired admitted.

"I do not approve of what you and my son did," Quintus said, "but it gave us Lupinus." Litana wasn't sure what Domina Maired had done that was so bad, but she was very happy they had Lupinus.

The rest of the day went quickly, Maired led Litana back to the domus and they packed all Maired's possessions. Quintus paid for a messenger to bring the trunk to the new home. Once it arrived Litana organized the shelves.

When the night came, they got Lupinus to bed and were about to start story time when there was a knock on the door. Litana answered the door and Prisca was standing in the corridor with a clay pot that was filled with something that smelled good. Litana invited her in.

"I brought some food," Prisca said, she pulled another codex of parchment out. "And this, another letter from Paulos. He is one of the best teachers we have."

"Thank you," Maired said, taking the codex. Litana hoped they would read it during story time. Prisca visited with them for a moment and then left.

Maired decided to start the new codex for story time. They read it while they ate the hot food. It was hard to understand sometimes, but Litana loved the way the words sounded. It all brought peace to her heart. As they finished, Litana got her mat to sleep on the floor.

"Why don't you sleep on the other bed?" Maired asked. Litana had never even considered it. She climbed into the bed and was amazed how comfortable it was. As she drifted off to sleep, she thought about what that nice lady had said, "all are the same in Iēsus."

Chapter 26
Taran

The big gates to the caupona were heavy and took effort to close after a long day. Taran and Ceredig always closed them before sending Ceredig home for the day. Once the bar was secured across the gate Taran could head to bed. He was tired and looking forward to some sleep. He checked the fire in the kitchen to make sure the coals were buried in ash.

Riva and Artor were sleeping in the big room with Maeli while she and Samira had the small room. Everyone was already asleep except Samira who was sitting on their bed nursing Nura. He smiled, he never saw himself as a family man, but now that he was, he wouldn't do anything else. Taran undressed for bed and lay with his wife. After Nura had nursed to sleep, they snuggled together and went to sleep.

A loud noise startled Taran. Samira was sitting up and turned to him with a puzzled look. Taran stood up and pulled on his tunic as the noise came again, it sounded like something was smashing against the wooden gate. He took his sword from a peg on the wall and took it from its sheath. "Bandits?" Samira asked.

"I don't know," Taran said. Only poor
bandits made this much noise at night. He
reached out and grabbed Samira's curved
sword and handed it to her. "Stay here with
Nura," Taran said as the banging continued,
"I'll go see what is happening." Taran knew
that Samira would protect Nura.

As Taran walked through the big
room, Artor and Riva were huddled together,
scared. After losing their home to raiders, they
must be terrified, Taran realized. Maeli was
standing with her own sword, waiting for
Taran. The two quietly walked down the
stairs. The banging was louder and coming
from the gates. Guests were in the courtyard
wondering what was going on.

Suddenly one of the gates shattered
and sprinters fell to the ground with a crash.
Roman legionaries started to rush through the
gate. There were so many of them that Taran
threw his sword down, he couldn't fight them.
He wasn't sure if he would need to. He
decided to take a stance.

"What is all this?" Taran demanded as
he saw a man wearing the uniform of a
Centurion. The Centurion was a smaller man
but carried himself with an air of authority.
"Why did you break down the gate?"

"I have come to arrest the caupo of
this caupona!" the Centurion exclaimed.

"On what charge?" Taran kept his demeanor rough. He was very upset that they would come here in the middle of the night and disturb him and his guests.

"Contempt of the gods," the Centurion said, "and insurrection against Ceasar!"

"How?" Taran demanded. "We are loyal to Ceasar."

"I have testimony that you are holding insurrectionist meetings here," the Centurion said. He was done talking and grabbed Taran. Maeli stepped forward and grabbed the Centurion's wrist.

"It's me you want," Maeli said, "he knows nothing of our meetings." Taran was about to object but his mother gave him a look. The look that tells a son not to contradict his mother. The Centurion released Taran and looked around, confused.

"I was told it was a man who ran these meetings," the Centurion said.

"You were told wrong," Maeli said firmly. The Centurion shook his head and looked around at the guests.

"Fine!" the Centurion finally said, "by your own admission I am arresting you." The Centurion grabbed Maeli and pushed her towards two legionaries who each took an arm. "This caupona is now shut down under

the order of Publius Metilius Nepos, governor
of Brittania!"

"You can't do that!" Maeli shouted.
The Centurion turned and slapped her face.
She fell backwards but was caught by the men
who were holding her. Taran was ready to
intervene when a hand touched his arm.
Samira had come down with the baby. Riva
and Artor were with them.

"Everyone is ordered to gather their
belongings and leave immediately!" the
Centurion shouted. There was a mad scramble
as the guests, used to Roman brutality, ran to
gather their things. Taran turned, but the
Centurion stopped him. "Not you, all of the
items in this caupona now belongs to Rome.
Leave now."

Samira gently pulled Taran through
the archway into the street. She kept walking
with her head low. Riva and Artor were close
behind.

"Don't look back," Samira said, "we
must go before they realize the money is
gone." Taran wasn't sure what they were
talking about but followed them to the path
that went to Seren and Owain's farm. He
could hear the sound of destruction. They
were smashing everything in his home.

"What about Ma?" Taran asked.

"She sacrificed herself for us," Samira said, "we must respect that." Taran was unsure what to do, he felt the need to go back and rescue his mother, but Samira was right. She had stopped forward to protect him. He respected that even if it took all his strength to keep him moving away from the caupona.

When they arrived at Owain and Seren's farm the world felt silent. They knocked on the door to the roundhouse, and a young man opened the door. He had light brown hair that was tangled from sleep and light brown eyes.

"Llyr," Taran said, "it's us, let us in." Seren's oldest boy Llyr opened the door and let them in. Owain was standing behind his son holding a spear. His dark eyes were barely visible in the low light. Seren got out of bed and rushed to them while Teleri thought of putting some wood on the fire. As the flames started to leap up the wood, they could see each other.

"What's going on?" Seren asked. Her normally cheerful face furrowed with concern.

"Romans came and arrested Ma," Taran said, "they are taking her away and have taken the caupona!" Seren couldn't take it all in, especially as Taran quickly told her what had happened. Owain finally put an arm on his wife's shoulder.

"It's late," Owain said, "they are tired, let them sleep. In the morning, I will go with Taran and find out what happened to Maeli." They all found places to sleep, most of them on the floor by the fire. Sleep did not come quickly as they each lay there wondering what was happening to Maeli.

The next morning everyone was sullen and the mood was tense. Even the little Artor seemed to sense it and sat quietly by the fire. Taran was sitting and trying to decide what his next move should be when there was a knock on the door. Seren answered it and Gaius came in.

"I thought I might find you here," Gaius said. He had been staying in the old slave quarters, and when the Romans attacked had hidden. "I pretended to be a guest and snuck away. I followed the legionaries to where they are keeping Maeli," he explained.

"Where is she?" Taran asked.

"She's being kept in a tent at the camp on the hill," Gaius said, "it's a good walk from here. I have alerted the Christians in the area. We will find a way to save her."

"I want to help," Taran said.

"It's better if you stay here," Gaius said, "they know you. We will get her; you take care of your family. They've destroyed your home; you need to care for your family."

Taran didn't like the idea of sitting here and waiting for someone to rescue his mother, but he also had to take care of Samira and Nura.

Gaius excused himself and rushed off to get his plan moving. The family sat there staring into the flames. Taran wondered what he should do now. He couldn't just wait until his mother was rescued. He tried to think of a plan, they needed something to keep them occupied.

"I think we need to see what they have done to the caupona," Taran said.

"Best if I go first," Owain said, "they don't know me. If any legionaries are left behind, they will think I am a curious neighbor."

"Be careful," Seren said. Owain put a hand on her shoulder.

"I will be," Owain said before kissing her and heading out. It was a tense few minutes of waiting until Owain came back to tell them the inn was unguarded. Seren offered to keep the children and they could all go inspect the damage.

Taran led the group along the path, with Samira close behind. He still didn't know what he would do if the caupona was destroyed. He knew he could go back to trading, but he always felt a connection to his home. It was family and history; he wanted Nura to know that history.

The arch still stood, but the sign was smashed, a single board left hanging off one of the hooks. The gate had a parchment nailed to it. Taran read it aloud.

"This caupona has been seized by the governor of Britannia Publius Metilius Nepos under the authority of Caesar Domitian Augustus, Emperor of Rome." Taran read, he turned to the rest of the family. "Let's see what we have left."

They walked through the broken gate to see that the courtyard was littered with linens and broken furniture. The doors to each cubiculum were open and it appeared that they had cleaned each room. The kitchen was a mess of broken pottery and food slathered everywhere. They had even smashed the wooden stalls in the stable.

Taran went to look at the rooms and each one was empty; they had emptied out the family quarters as well. Taran realized they had been looking for the money. During the confusion, Samira had snuck into the tablinium and taken the purse of coins. She had hidden it in her skirts before coming to him.

"It's ruined," Owain said, "I'm so sorry."

"I guess it belongs to Rome now,"
Taran said softly. "We need to find a new way
to live."

Chapter 27
Maeli

The tent in the camp was small and drafty. Maeli wished she had grabbed her cloak before coming down the stairs, she was only wearing her under tunic. She tried to keep warm by curling up on the mat they had given her, but it wasn't working. She lay there shivering.

She still believed she had done the right thing. She had been the one to insist the meetings continue after Quintus left for Rome. He had promised to bring back a message from Maired, now she likely would never hear about her daughter. She wondered if the baby was a boy or a girl.

Maeli had appreciated the teaching of Iēsus. It made sense to her that instead of a bunch of gods that nobody could see, there was one God that sent a part of himself to the world. As a child the gods seemed to abandon her, and now she knew why, they weren't the right god. She lived for the meetings, and now she would likely die for them too.

"Iēsus," Maeli said softly, "I would just like to see my daughter one last time." The tent flap opened and a legionary walked in and grabbed her arm. He pulled her to her feet and dragged her out to the middle of the camp where a platform had been set up. On the platform was a shrine to one of the Roman gods, the Centurion who had arrested her was standing in front of the shrine.

"You have been accused of teaching a god other than the true gods of Rome," the Centurion said, "if you make a sacrifice to the god Vesta I will release you." Maeli considered for a moment; how hard would it be to bake some bread and leave it on an altar? She then thought about the discussions they had about Adonai. Gaius had shared that Adonai had laws against making sacrifices to other gods. She did not want to go against Adonai or Iēsus, even if it made things easier.

"I refuse," Maeli said. She looked out among the people watching her. They were mostly legionaries, but there were a few people who were obviously from the surrounding area. She was startled for a moment when she saw Marcus in the crowd. He looked upset, he turned and walked away from the crowd.

The Centurion stepped towards Maeli and without another word slapped her face so hard she stumbled backwards. She felt a rage flow through her she had not felt since she was a slave. She stood up straight, she would never sacrifice to a Roman god! It didn't matter what he threatened to do to her.

"What are you doing?" a voice called from the crowd. Maeli looked out and saw a man she had never seen before. He was older, had a bald head and his skin was pale. He was wearing a Roman toga instead of a tunic. He did not fit in with this crowd. Maeli could see that the Centurion knew this man.

"Domine," the Centurion said, "she has rejected our gods."

"Did you give her a chance to speak?" The man asked.

"I gave her a chance to demonstrate loyalty," the Centurion said. "She has plainly rejected Vesta; her actions speak for her."

"Let her speak," the man said, he looked straight at Maeli and asked, "have you ever been to Rome?" Maeli wasn't sure why that mattered but answered honestly.

"I have Domine," Maeli said slowly, her face expressing her confusion. There was a rumble of talk among the crowd. The Centurion demanded silence.

"Did you ever visit the forum?" the old man asked. Maeli thought back to the day that her old Domina, Druscilla, had granted her freedom.

"Yes, Domine," Maeli said, "the day I was freed from being a slave." The legionaries started to lose discipline and talk amongst themselves. The Centurion was too shocked to ask for silence; he stood for a moment trying to figure out what that might mean before calling for silence again.

"Were you granted citizenship with your manumission?" Maeli knew that she had been made a citizen of Rome on that day. It had never really mattered to her, so she didn't think about it much.

"Domine Centurion," the man said, "as a citizen of Rome, this woman is under my authority as procurator. Release her to me at once."

"The charges still remain," the Centurion said.

"Yes," the man said, "and she will face those charges in Rome." The Centurion had nothing else to say. Maeli had heard before that a Roman citizen had a right to be heard in the forum if accused of a crime. While that technically applied to her, she never would have considered it.

This bought her time, and possibly with a different person she could appeal and be released. The legionary who brought her here led her back to the tent, gently this time. Once she was in the tent, the bald man came in and handed her a cloak. She immediately recognized it as one belonging to Gaius.

"Our friend wanted you to have this," the old man said, "no need to ask about him."

It was a warning not to talk; there would be people listening. "My name is Aulus Plautus," as he spoke, he was drawing something on the ground with his toe. Maeli realized it was a fish symbol. The symbol of Iēsus, he was a follower of the way!

"What will happen next?" Maeli asked.

"I will take you to Rome," Aulus said firmly.

"What about my family?" Maeli thought about Taran and Samira and the baby. They would be able to manage without her. So she moved on before he could answer with her real concern. "What happened to my caupona?"

"I have seized the caupona," Aulus said, "your son has also been accused of holding meetings by a witness, but he has disappeared." Maeli hoped he would manage to stay hiding.

Aulus gently grabbed her arm and pulled her from the tent. There were legionaries all around, but Maeli did not see Marcus anywhere. She followed Aulus through the camp and down the steep hill. Once they were out of sight, Aulus released Maeli.

"Is it safe to talk?" Maeli asked softly.

"This is the only safe place," Aulus said. There were a few people walking on the cobblestone road, but they were not paying any attention to the two walking from the camp.

"Who are you?" Maeli asked.

"I am who I said I am," Aulus said, "I am the procurator for this region, I seize land and arrest people for not paying taxes. I have the authority to put the caupona in my list of properties."

"I see," Maeli said. He had not told her what she wanted to know. She wanted to know why he was here.

"I'm also a friend of Gaius," Aulus added, "we have a network of Roman believers that can help when needed. It's a small network but growing."

"He called you," Maeli said, thankful that her friend had helped.

"He did," Aulus said. "We are going to get too close to town to talk, so let me tell you what will happen next. I will take you to Rome, I have no choice. Once we are there, a friend of yours will help you." Maeli wondered what friend in Rome he was referring to. "You will go into hiding until we can safely bring you back. Gaius will tell your son."

"That is all we can do?" Maeli asked.

"I am bound by the law," Aulus said.

They had reached the town of
Isurium, which was a small Roman town.
There were some buildings with columns to
emulate the bigger buildings in Rome, some
temples and
insulae. Other buildings were in the Briton
style, wooden and plain. They walked to the
forum, a building with a large courtyard and
columned corridors. Maeli could tell they tried
to copy the one she had visited in Rome.

Aulus took her to a small room in the
back where she was given a place to sleep and
some food. She was locked in, a prisoner. The
next few weeks went quickly. She was taken
from that small room the next day and moved
to Londinium. From there she was put on a
boat and taken to Gaul, and on to Rome.

All she could think about was her
family. She wondered what Taran would do
without the caupona to earn money. She
wondered if she would ever see him again.
When she arrived in Rome her mind shifted
to Maired. She was now in the same city as
her daughter, that was the only positive thing
about any of this.

When she arrived in the big city, she
was escorted by a legionary down a narrow
alley to a small door. He opened the door and
inside was the Centurion Quintus Tiberius.
Maeli stopped in her tracks; she couldn't

believe what she was seeing. He stood there in a narrow corridor with all the authority he might have on a battlefield.

"Think you lad," Quintus said, "in an hour you will report to me that she escaped." The legionary smiled and raised his arm in salute. After he left, Quintus led Maeli down the corridor to a staircase. They climbed up and came back a short way along the upper corridor. There was a door partially open and Quintus opened it.

In the room was Maired holding her baby. Maeli rushed in and hugged her daughter. Tears ran down her face as she held her little girl.

Part III

Escape into the
future

5 years later

Chapter 28
Taran

The arch still stood in the same place, strong and resolute against the destruction all around it. Taran pushed away some of the wood that was left from the gate and entered the courtyard. Artor, now eight years old, with his pale hair and line of freckles across his nose, held his hand as they walked in.

It was strange, because it looked the same, but different. It was all there, the guest rooms, the entrance to the bathhouse, the big kitchen. Everything was falling apart and nature had started to take over. The walls were covered with vines and there were a few small trees scattered in the courtyard.

"This will take some work," Taran said to Artor.

"I'll help," Artor said bravely. These last few years Artor and Riva had joined Taran and Samira in Petra where they had established a trading company. When Roman trade routes changed, their business dried up and they decided to return to Britannia.

Taran had bribed a magistrate in Londinium to release the caupona back to him. He hoped now that he had enough money left to get the building back into shape. He needed something to pass on to his children. Nura was five years old and a great big sister to her brothers Ramon and Malik.

Artor wandered around looking at the courtyard, he disappeared into the old stable and came back a moment later. The boy was as brave as any boy Taran had seen, he was exploring this new environment without any fear.

There was a sound behind him and Taran turned to see Ceredig and Teleri coming through the arch. The couple had married shortly before Taran's return and newlywed life seemed to suit them.

"Ma told me you were back," Teleri said. "We thought we would come and offer our help."

"Thank you," Taran said, "I will need it." He and Ceredig walked around discussing the different tasks that would need to be done. The roof of the inn was almost completely gone and there was a lot of damage to the walls. He would need to hire a carpenter and a mason. That would take a lot of his money.

With a plan in place the four of them returned to the roundhouse where everyone was staying. It was the home of Seren and Owain and was very crowded, but Seren had insisted that they stay with her. Samira saw Taran's expression when he entered the house and knew that it was not good. They had been business partners for long enough, she knew he would discuss all expenses with her.

Taran sat by the hearth and Nura climbed into his lap. He played with her brown hair; in the firelight it looked more red than brown. He went through the expected costs in his head, but the time he got the caupona running, he would have to fill it with guests immediately. There would be no money to live on if they didn't.

Samira sat with Taran and waited patiently for him to think. She knew that he would come to her when he needed someone else to help him find a solution, that was how they worked as a team. Finally, he turned to her and smiled.

"There is almost too much to do," Taran said. "I should have come here before bribing the magistrate. I might have changed my mind about trying to restart the caupona."

"Tomorrow we will start," Samira said, "everyone is willing to help. We will find a way. Remember when the bandits attacked? We worked together and won. We will work together. We will win."

The next morning Taran and Artor helped milk the cows and then the whole family walked together to the caupona. They decided they needed to get the plants out of the courtyard and vines off the walls first. Artor and Nura ran around the courtyard pulling up small plants and giggling. Ramon joined in but went for the saplings that were too big.

Taran's mood lightened as he helped his son pull up the small trees. He noticed Ceredig and Llyr working together to take what remained of the gate off the hinges. Llyr was almost twenty-four years old, Taran wondered why he wasn't betrothed or married yet. He mentioned the observation to Samira as they worked to help Ramon with one of the saplings.

"Owain cannot find a family that will let him marry their daughter," Samira said softly. "Seren told me yesterday, everyone thinks they will make any wife of his reject their gods."

"Poor Llyr," Taran said. "He's a good man; he would make a great husband." They kept working until the sun was starting to go down. Owain had left with Llyr to care for the cows while they looked around at the progress.

Most of the plants were uprooted and the vines were off the walls. Taran and Samira walked around to get a better look at what else needed to be done. The first cubiculum in the line did not look too bad, there was water damage to the plaster, and the roof was completely gone. The second cubiculum still had a roof, so the water damage was less. The final guest cubiculum was the worst. The wall between the room and the bathhouse was starting to fall.

The bathhouse was completely ruined. This is what upset Taran the most. The mosaic floor of the changing room was torn up and the roof was completely gone. There were a few walls still partially standing, but most were collapsed.

The stable needed to be completely rebuilt, but at least the walls were intact. Taran couldn't believe so much damage could be done in five years. The kitchen had the worst damage. The living quarters above the kitchen had collapsed into it.

"We can rebuild all of this," Samira said. Taran nodded, they could, but at what cost?

Chapter 29
Maired

Maired was lying in bed when she heard a noise in the hall. The door was opening; she leapt out of bed and rushed to the front room. The insula she was in was bigger than the one in the community of

Christians. Marcus had objected to her living there and paid for her to have this bigger place. He had visited her a few times and then would go back to his military life. She was always happy to see him leave.

The front door was opening; Maeli had also come out of her cubiculum. Marcus entered the cenaculum, the main room of the three-room apartment, and Maired let out a sigh. She wondered if it would have been easier if it was an intruder and regretted the thought. She should be thankful her husband was home; she forced herself to smile.

"Welcome home," Maired said. Marcus looked around the insula, looking for some fault. Maired tried not to think the worst of him, but he always criticized her when he came home.

"Where's my son?" Marcus asked. Lupinus came into the room and immediately hid behind his mother. It had been over a year since he had seen his father and didn't know who he was. Marcus got down to greet his son, but Lupinus hid his face. Marcus stood again, obviously upset that his son didn't want to greet him.

Maired wanted to ask when he was leaving but felt that would sound like she wished he was gone already. She would have to be careful what she said, he would eventually tell her. Maeli took Lupinus by the hand and brought him out of hiding,

"Let's give your father a hug," Maeli said softly, "then let Ma and Da talk." Lupinus obeyed his grandmother and hugged Marcus before going with her into another room. After they were gone Marcus kissed Maired lightly.

"He's getting big," Marcus said.

"He is," Maired said.

"Where is your girl?" Marcus asked. "I need her to bring my belongings in." Maired called Litana who must have been hiding. Litana did not like Marcus' visits and usually spent all her time hiding. Litana carried Marcus' trunk in from the corridor and placed it into the cubiculum. She started to unpack it without further instruction.

"Let her work," Maired said, "I'll get you some ale." Marcus followed her into the other room, and they sat together while he drank.

"How are you?" Maired asked her husband.

"I'm doing well," Marcus said, "I'm being transferred to the praetorian guard. It means more pay and I will be home in Rome." Maired felt all the air leave her. She couldn't believe that he would be staying. She put another smile on her face.

"That's good news," Maired said, "you will be able to spend more time with Lupinus. He will be happy about that." Marcus looked towards the room where Maeli had taken Lupinus.

"Yes," Marcus said. Maired could tell by his expression that he was upset about something. Then she realized that he did not like her mother. She would likely need to move out if he lived here. Maired was not happy with that idea, but it might be necessary to keep the peace. Ever since her mother showed up five years ago, life had been a little easier.

Maeli had been a strong presence in the home, especially when Marcus was home. She gave Maired the strength she needed to put up with Marcus. She would speak with her mother after a while, and they could decide together what to do. She was not about to let Marcus be the one to make that decision. If Maeli wanted to stay, they would just deal with it.

"I'm going to make sure that fool girl doesn't mess anything up," Marcus said, going to the cubiculum. Maired rushed to her mother.

"He's staying," Maired announced as soon as she entered the room.

"I see," Maeli said, she was playing a game of knucklebones with Lupinus. The goal was to throw all four bones in the air and catch them all on the back of your hand. Lupinus was in the middle of his turn and stopped to listen to the women.

"Who's staying?" Lupinus asked.

"Your father," Maired answered, "he's going to be a legionary here in Rome." Lupinus' eyes lit up, Maired had always talked positively about Marcus to her son. He needed a father he could look up to the way she looked up to her own father. She hoped they would have a positive relationship.

"That's good," Lupinus said. He jumped up and rushed out of cubiculum, Maired close behind. They went to Maired's cubiculum. As they walked through the door, Marcus jumped as they rushed in. Maired felt like he looked guilty for a second. Litana rushed out of the room to give them privacy.

"Lupinus is excited you will be staying," Maired explained as Lupinus leapt into his father's arms.

"Yeah!" Lupinus said, "Ma says you're the bravest man in the legion!" Marcus looked at Maired with a confused gaze.

"It's important he knows about his father," Maired said. "It will be good to have you home for a while." She was trying to convince herself, maybe it would be better if he was living with them. He was good with Lupinus, he always had been. He enjoyed being a father.

Maired left father and son to catch up. She needed to organize some food for the family. They had a small space in this insula to prepare food, but no fire so if they wanted hot food, she would have to buy it. There was a Caupona nearby that sold good food. This morning, they would have cold bread and cheese with some smoked meat. To celebrate Marcus' return, she decided they would buy some hot food for the evening meal.

The family reclined at the table to eat, Lupinus insisted that he be next to his father. Litana served the food and went to the corner of the room to wait for her turn to eat. When it was just the ladies, she ate with them, but Marcus insisted she behave appropriately for her status. Maired did notice that he kept checking to make sure she stayed in her place. Or was it something else? Litana looked like she was upset with him looking at her.

Maired looked at Litana from a different perspective. She had not really realized that the girl had become a woman. She was still as simple as a child and likely would remain that way, but her body was a woman's body. Maired realized too that her simple slave's tunic emphasized some of her curves. She wondered if Marcus was noticing that too.

When the meal finished Marcus announced that he was required to report to the Castra Praetoria as soon as he could. He told Maired he would be home soon, kissed Lupinus and was gone. Litana got to work with cleaning up.

"Lupinus," Maeli said, "you go outside to play, I'll be out soon." Lupinus didn't need to be told twice, he jumped up and rushed outside to play. There were other children in the building, and he had friends he would find and play with. As soon as he was gone Maeli called Litana back into the room.

"Yes Domina?" Litana asked as she came in.

"Tell Domina Maired what you told me," Maeli said softly. Litana's eyes dropped to the floor and she shook her head. "She won't be upset," Maeli said gently. Maired wondered what the girl had broken this time. It was a common occurrence, but Litana was always embarrassed about doing it.

"When I was helping Domine Marcus," Litana said softly, so she had broken something of his, Maired thought. He would be upset unless she could replace it quickly. "When I was helping him," Litana started

202

again, talking slowly, "he rubbed me down there." She looked down towards her groin.

Maired took a moment to realize what she was saying. Litana was staring at the floor and Maeli's face was turning red. Maired took a deep breath and tried to think of what to say.

"He did this on purpose?" Maired asked and then realized the stupidity of the question. Of course it was on purpose, that was not something you could do accidentally. "Has he ever done anything like this before?" Maired asked before Litana could answer the first question.

"He likes to touch people," Litana said, "but you don't like it. I wasn't supposed to tell you. I'm sorry." Maired realized that this poor girl had been terrorized by Marcus this whole time.

"She told me because I saw her crying," Maeli said, "and made her tell." Maeli was angry, which Maired understood.

"I'm not angry with you," Maired said, "you did nothing wrong. You don't like being touched, do you?"

"No," Litana said, "I don't. But he says he owns me and not to tell you because he can do what he wants." Litana sniffed. "He said you would be jealous because he likes me better. But I don't want him to, please don't be angry."

"I'm not angry," Maired said. She was angry, angry enough to envision her husband lying dead on the ground with her standing over him with a spear. "Can you go make sure Lupinus is keeping out of trouble?" Litana's face lit up, watching Lupinus was her favorite job. She rushed out the door; she had been rewarded instead of punished.

"We need to get her away from that man as soon as possible," Maeli said.

"Agreed," Maired said, "but how?"

"She's your slave, not his," Maeli pointed out. "You can give her to someone."

"She would see that as punishment," Maired said, "and he would become suspicious and might get her back." Maired thought back to her illicit relationship with him, he did not stop once he decided he liked a woman.

"We need to get her out of Rome," Maeli said, "and in a way he won't think suspicious." Maired realized what the only solution would be.

"Ma," Maired said softly, "I need you to take her away." Maeli's face went from concern to determination. "It's the only thing that makes sense. Marcus would be happy to see you leave and won't question you taking someone to help." It was the best solution for Litana, even though it would leave Maired alone with the monster she called husband.

Chapter 30
Llyr

The stone mason had worked quickly to get the walls back into place. Llyr had learned a lot from him as he helped with the work. They had built the walls by fitting stones together and filling the gaps with small stones and mortar. Llyr had enjoyed mixing the lime and sand with water.

By helping Llyr had helped the family save money on rebuilding. Getting away from the cows was an added benefit. He didn't mind the cows, but it was fun to do something new.

Taran came into the courtyard as Llyr was mixing more mortar and inspected the work that had been done. He seemed happy, which was good. Llyr had sensed how stressed his cousin was. He was only two years younger than Taran but felt so much less experienced. Taran had found a wife in another country. Llyr wondered if he would ever get the opportunity to do the same.

"Once we are done with this wall, we can start setting up the kitchen," Taran said as he came closer.

"I'll let Tegid know," Llyr said. He had been able to get his friend to agree to do the carpentry work for the promise of free meals once the caupona opened. Taran thanked him and walked over to where Samira had the children working on making baskets. The baskets she made were good enough to store grains. It would mean saving money on pots.

Llyr was impressed at how Taran found ways to save money. He had finished mixing the mortar and informed the mason that he had an errand to run and would be back. The trail to Tegid's house took him across the green fields. He loved to look across the rolling hills, he thought again about going somewhere else to find a wife and wondered if it would be worth leaving his beautiful home.

Tegid lived alone in his roundhouse on the far side of the village. He had been married, but his wife died in childbirth and he was left alone. He told Llyr that he honestly preferred not having a woman telling him when to be home and what to do. Llyr imagined he said that to make him feel better about not having a wife.

"Llyr," Tegrid said as he walked up, "how is our caupona doing?" Most of the villagers considered the caupona to be a part of the village, the loss of it had hurt them all financially.

"It's coming," Llyr said, "Taran said we can start on the kitchen tomorrow and then the roof after that." Tegrid nodded, he was not new to carpentry, as the son of a carpenter his whole life had revolved around it. However, most of the village had never seen his work and were reluctant to hire him. Seeing his craftsmanship in the caupona would show his skills to everyone.

"I'll be there at first light," Tegrid said. "You must be thirsty, join me in a drink before heading home." Llyr had time and sat with his friend to drink some ale. They discussed the community news and shared about what various friends were doing.

Llyr had often discussed his frustrations with the lack of betrothal with Tegrid. Like a true friend Tegrid had encouraged him that eventually people would forget the past.

"One good thing," Tegrid said, "is that the caupona will help the community get past what happened."

"I hope so," Llyr said, "if not I may have to go to Gaza or Petra like Taran did."

"His wife is beautiful," Tegrid said.

"She's a good wife too," Llyr said, "you should taste some of the food she cooks."

"I'm looking forward to doing that," Tegrid said with a laugh. As the sun started to set, Llyr started home. Walking across his way back across the hills, wondering how Taran ever left, even if it did help him find a wife.

Chapter 31
Maired

Marcus had agreed it would be a good thing for Maeli to head back to Brittania. He was visibly upset when Maired had told him that she was sending Litana with her. She had explained that her mother was getting older and needed someone to help her. She did not express her suspicion that he was mistreating her.

Maired hated saying goodbye to her mother and her slave who had become her best friend. She sat alone in her insula with Lupinus. At least she had come to enjoy his company. She didn't dote on him like her mother did, or help him do things like Litana did, but she could enjoy being with him. He was the biggest loser in all of this, stuck here with a mother who tolerated him and losing the two who loved him. Maired looked at his shaggy dark hair and his dark eyes.

He had wept all during the goodbyes and now he was playing alone with his game. Maired sat down on the floor with him and picked up a bone. She knew how this game worked, she practiced throwing it up and catching it. Lupinus looked at her and grinned.

"No, Ma," Lupinus said in an irritated tone, "you have to toss all four." Maired laughed despite herself and took all four and tried again. She missed two of them, this game was not as easy as it looked.

"Your turn," Maired said. Lupinus tossed the bones and caught them all. He giggled as Maired cheered for him. He tried again and missed one. It was Maired's turn.

The game continued for a while and Maired improved a little. Lupinus was enjoying the time with his mother and Maired found she was enjoying it too. The door opened and Maired realized she had lost track of time. Marcus walked in looking handsome in his uniform. Lupinus jumped up and ran to him.

Marcus hugged his son then turned back to the corridor and dragged in a young girl. She looked to be about sixteen or seventeen years old. She was short and skinny with stringy blonde hair and the palest blue eyes Maired had seen. Her skin was almost translucent, as was the tunic she was wearing. Maired recognized it immediately as one from the slave market.

"I got a replacement for you," Marcus said. Maired didn't know if he meant she was to replace Litana or herself. Whichever it was,

she was not happy he had bought another
slave without talking with her.

"What's her name?" Maired asked,
reaching for the girl.

"I don't know," Marcus said, "she was
all I could afford. You gave away the one that
spoke Latin. This one doesn't speak a word. I
guess you will have to deal with that." Maired
glared at Marcus.

"I'm going to get her settled," Maired
gently pulled the girl into her cubiculum.
Marcus was following which angered Maired
more, but she didn't dare say anything. "I was
going to buy some food at the caupona, why
don't you take Lupinus for food and I'll eat
something here." Marcus stopped; he glanced
towards Lupinus.

"Fine," Marcus said. "She better be
settled quickly."

"You bought her!" Maired said
angrily, "I hadn't planned on doing anything
with a new slave."

"I thought you would be happy,"
Marcus said, the anger in his voice bothered
Maired. She let out a snort, happy that he had
brought another girl in here? She wondered
what went on in his mind. She shook her head
and took the girl away from Marcus. She
heard the front door slam shut and checked to
be sure her husband was gone.

The poor girl was petrified; she stood in the middle of the room with her eyes down and arms down in front of her, gently wringing her hands. Marcus had mentioned that she didn't speak Latin, Maired wondered if she understood the old tongue of the Britons. She decided to try something.

"Do you have a name?" Maired asked. The girls' eyes flickered with recognition, she at least understood something.

She lifted her eyes and said, "Yrsa." She said it so softly Maired barely heard her.

"Yrsa?" Maired asked and the girl nodded. "I'm Maired, you will need to learn to call me Domina." Yrsa nodded, she seemed to be understanding a little of what Maired was saying. A terrible thought crossed her mind, Maired wondered if Marcus had brought this girl home because she couldn't tell anyone what he was doing to her.

"Do you understand me?" Maired asked. Yrsa stood staring at the ground again. She tried again, "do you know my words?" but the girl still stared at the floor. Maired decided she couldn't really talk to the girl after all. She had probably been taught a few useful Latin words like "Domina" on her way to Rome.

Maired left the girl alone for a moment and looked around for a tunic that

might fit the girl. The current one did little for
the girl's modesty, Maired was determined
that she be covered when Marcus next saw
her. She found one of Litana's old tunics, the
first one she had bought her years ago. It
would go down to this girl's feet, but that
would work for today.

Maired showed Yrsa the clean tunic
and then pointed at the old one. She pinched
her nose and made a face, which got a smile
out of Yrsa. She handed the new tunic to
Yrsa, who took off her old tunic to put the
clean one on. Maired was shocked at how thin
the girl was, her ribs were poking through the
skin on her side. Her little stomach stuck out
a little with made her look more sickly than
anything.

"Maybe he did just buy you to help,"
Maired said aloud, she couldn't imagine he
found this girl to be attractive. She looked
into the blue eyes; they were the same color as
the sky. That must have been what he saw, he
was thinking of having this beautiful girl
around the house once she was healthy.
Maired felt pure hatred for her husband.

With the tunic on, Maired took Yrsa
to get some food. She remembered her
mother talking about hating rich Roman food
when she had been a slave, so Maired pulled
out some bread and cheese for the girl. Her

eyes grew as she looked at the food. Maired wondered what she had been eating since being taken as a slave.

As the girl finished wolfing down her food, the door opened and Lupinus rushed into the insula. He had a variety of stains on the front of his tunic. Marcus followed closely behind. He looked Yrsa over and then approached Maired.

"She's not very clean," Marcus said.

"I'm going to let her get used to me before I clean her up," Maired said sternly. Lupinus rushed over to them and asked who the new girl was.

"She's the new slave," Marcus said, "I told you about her."

"Oh yeah," Lupinus said before going to the girl and trying to introduce himself.

"She doesn't speak our language," Maired explained. "Her name is Yrsa."

"I'll never be able to say that" Marcus said, "call her Caesia." This reinforced Maired's suspicion that her eyes were what attracted Marcus to her; he wanted to call her "blue eyes."

"I will call her by her name until she has learned our language," Maired said, "why confuse the girl?" Marcus obviously did not expect her to talk back in this way. His face went red, but his tone was calm and level.

"Fine," Marcus said, "do it your way." He stormed into their cubiculum. Maired then noticed that Lupinus was leading Yrsa by the hand into his cubiculum. She let them go and a moment later heard giggling from the doorway. Apparently, they didn't need to be able to talk to play.

Chapter 32
Maeli

Maeli looked up at the arch that led to her husband's caupona. She remembered the first time she saw this archway; she was a slave being dragged here to see the boy that sold her. She ended up marrying that boy. He had bought her at the slave market to rescue her and take her to a household where she would end up being treated well. Neither of them realized at the time that they would have a good life together.

The sign with the triskelion symbol was not hanging and there were people climbing on the roof. Were they renovating? Litana was keeping behind her out of habit, although Maeli told her to stop acting like a slave. She was a free person in this land.

"They must be fixing it up," Maeli said. That meant business had been good. Litana looked at the big building with its big arch and smiled at Maeli.

"It is very big," Litana said, "you own all this?" Maeli nodded.

"My family does," Maeli said. "My husband's parents owned it first." Litana looked impressed. Maeli liked that she was easy to impress, she might act simple sometimes, but she was a good friend.

Maeli led Litana through the arch into the courtyard which was a hive of activity. Men were working with clay tiles, carrying them to the roof. From here she could see a few changes, new doors, a new kitchen layout and a bigger stone oven. Finally, a familiar face appeared, Llyr, Seren and Owain's oldest. His light brown hair that fell gently across his face made him stand out in this crowd.

"Llyr," Maeli called out. Llyr turned to her and his jaw dropped. He rushed over to her and wrapped his arms around her.

"We thought you were dead!" Llyr said, which made Litana laugh. Llyr pulled back from the hug, "who is this?"

"This is Litana," Maeli said, "she's come to stay with us." Llyr bowed his head to her and then turned back to Maeli.

"We need to find Taran," Llyr said excitedly. "He's around somewhere!" Llyr rushed off before Maeli could say anything. She just stood there with Litana.

"He's funny," Litana said.

"He's the son of my husband's sister," Maeli explained, "he's always looked for the happier side of things."

"That's good," Litana said. Llyr returned with Taran close behind. When Taran saw his mother, he rushed to her and held her. He was weeping quietly, his face a mix of joy and despair. Llyr put his hand on Litana's arm.

"Let's leave them alone," Llyr said, "I'll show you around." Before Maeli could say anything Llyr had led her friend off to explore the caoupona.

"He hasn't changed," Maeli said with a chuckle.

"Where have you been?" Taran asked.

"Rome," Maeli said, "with your sister." Maeli told Taran a short version of the story, how she had been rescued by the Centurion Quintus and hid in a Christian community. Taran had questions about his sister and what was going on in her life.

Finally, Maeli asked about the renovations and Taran told her what they had done over the last five years. Maeli felt bad that her actions had driven them from their home for years, but Taran seemed content with the renovations.

"You can see," Taran said, leading Maeli on a tour, "we have improved the kitchen and rebuilt the bathhouse." The bathhouse was now bigger and had a better layout. They had put a corridor along the side that led into the various rooms. It also had smaller rooms that would be easier to heat. The corridor also meant that heat would not escape into the other rooms.

Maeli was impressed with all the work. She followed her son around and finally they came across Artor and Nura who were busy weaving more baskets. They were selling them in the market now, they were not as good as the ones Samira made, but the locals loved them.

"Nura," Taran said, "this is my mother." The little girl jumped up and hugged Maeli immediately. Now it was Maeli's turn to weep as she held the little girl she had helped bring into the world. "She has two younger brothers now," Taran said proudly. Maeli smiled at her as she picked up Nura.

"Let's go meet them," Maeli said to her son. Taran led her to Seren's roundhouse where Samira was watching the boys. It was a special time together as she played with Ramon and Malik. It was getting late then Maeli suddenly realized she had no idea where Litana was. She left the roundhouse to rush back to the caupona.

Litana was in the kitchen helping Teleri and Llyr organize the shelves. Maeli watched for a moment, she was fitting in and laughing with the two. There was a moment when Litana seemed a bit lost where to put a stack of clay plates and Llyr just took them from her and placed them on a shelf.

"It didn't take long for you to find something to do," Maeli said. Litana turned, she had a big smile on her face.

"Domina Teleri asked for help," Litana said. "This is a nice caupona. Can I stay and help?"

"I told you," Teleri said gently, "I am just Teleri. I'm not a Domina of anything." Litana looked a little embarrassed that she had forgotten.

"It's a hard habit to change," Maeli said, "she had to show respect to everyone in Rome. This isn't Rome, this is home." Litana smiled at the idea that she was home.

"I hope you can stay and help," Llyr said, "you've been helpful."

"We will have to find a place for you two to stay," Taran said with a smile. He was happy that his mother was home. They had changed the layout of the family quarters of the caupona. There would be three rooms, one for Riva and Artor, one for Taran and Samira and one for their children.

"The roof should be done in a few days," Llyr said, "until then you will all stay with us. Mother wouldn't want it any other way," Maeli knew he was right, she didn't want to impose, but they were family. They always helped each other.

Chapter 33
Maired

Yrsa was starting to gain weight, after weeks of feeding her healthy food. Maired still could not get the girl to understand her Latin, but she and Lupinus found a way to communicate and would play every day.

Marcus was expected to spend most of his nights at the castra praetoria. He was rarely home but came home some evenings to eat and play with Lupinus. Every few weeks he would have a day or two at home. Maired had almost forgotten her suspicions of Marcus' intentions as he seemed to ignore the girl completely. She dared to hope that the girl could stay.

Without Litana, Maired did most of the cleaning and other tasks. Yrsa was little help, but she kept Lupinus occupied which was good. Maired had bought her a nice dress that fit her small form. It was undyed wool but had a blue linen trim around the neck. She had beamed when Maired gave it to her. Maired was watching a game, sitting to mend some clothes, when a knock came at the door. Maired answered and Prisca was standing in the corridor.

"What brings you here?" Maired asked after Prisca had been invited to recline.

"I was in the area," Prisca said, "and I felt like coming by to see my old friend."

"I'm glad you're here," Maired said, "with my mother gone and a slave that doesn't speak Latin, I miss good conversation." Prisca gave a small laugh and looked over at the pale girl. Prisca had been told that Maeli was leaving and visited shortly before she left.

"She is so pretty," Prisca said, "do you have any idea where she came from?"

"I have a neighbor who once had a slave who looked similar," Maired said, "she said hers came from somewhere in Germania."

"That makes sense," Prisca said. "I was thinking about your concerns about your husband." Maired shook her head, Lupinus might listen and report what he heard to Marcus.

"Lupinus," Maired said, "why don't you two go out and buy some sweet bread?" Lupinus jumped up and grabbed Yrsa's hand. Maired handed the boy a copper coin, and he rushed out the door, dragging poor Yrsa behind him.

Once they were done Prisca continued, "I have asked discreetly for advice, there is not much you can do."

"What do you mean?" Maired asked.

"We know you can't divorce him," Prisca said, "the law would take your son and leave the girl in his charge."

"I'm not doing that." Maired had asked before about divorce, but the law gave everything to Marcus, she had come into the marriage with nothing. She didn't want to lose what little she had now.

"If you ran away," Prisca continued, "he could have you captured and brought back."

"I know," Maired wasn't sure she wanted to do that either. "I was thinking I needed to find a new home for Yrsa."

"She's his property," Prisca said, "Litana was given to you so he couldn't stop you giving her away. It's different with Yrsa. What remains is prayer."

"Prayer?" Maired asked. She knew what prayer was, talking to Adonai and Iēsus. No sacrifice or shrine, just sitting and talking to them. It was an odd concept for Maired, but Prisca seemed so sure of herself.

"I'm praying for your husband to have a change of heart," Prisca said. "I think that's the best solution." Maired wasn't convinced but appreciated Prisca for trying something. The door flew open and Lupinus and Yrsa returned with their treats in ther hands.

"Ma," Lupinus said loudly, "Yrsa has something to say!" Maired looked at the two wondering what they were up to. Yrsa held her bread in front of her.

"Thank you Domina," Yrsa said haltingly. Lupinus was smiling proudly.

"You're welcome;" Maired said softly. Yrsa turned to Lupinus and said something in her language, to Maired's surprise Lupinus responded in the same tongue. Somehow in all their playing, Lupinus had learned how to talk with her. Prisca let out a laugh.

"They are teaching each other," Prisca said, "isn't that amazing."

"It is," Maired said, watching the two eat their food and talking back and forth. She had not realized her son was learning to speak another tongue.

Prisca stayed a little longer and they shared other news from the community. Maired was distracted the entire time, watching Lupinus and Yrsa play. When Prisca left, Maired joined the two children.

"Lupinus," Maired said, "how much of what Yrsa says do you understand?"

"A little bit;" Lupinus said, "she has different words for everything."

"You've been teaching her Latin?" Maired asked.

"A little," Lupinus responded. "She wants to talk to you. She thinks you are nice." Maired realized she had not really been nice to the girl. She should be trying to teach her to speak and fit in here. The girl was stuck here with no hope for a future, the least she could do would be to teach her a few things.

"What words does she know?" Maired asked. Lupinus smiled and said something to Yrsa in her own language. Yrsa sat up tall and looked up at the ceiling.

"Yes, please, thank you, Domina," Yrsa said. Maired realized she was listing the words she knew, "knuckle, game, funny, bottom, fart." Maired then realized the problem with having a five-year-old boy teaching a girl to speak his language. Lupinus started to laugh and Maired joined him. Yrsa looked very proud of herself.

"Good," Maired said, nodding her head to show she approved. "Can you help me teach her words that are better for helping around the insula?" Lupinus nodded vigorously.

"Yes," Lupinus said. He turned to Yrsa and mixed the two languages together to explain to her what they were going to do. Yrsa smiled and nodded too.

The rest of the afternoon was spent finding things that were simple words and helping Yrsa learn to pronounce the word and associate it with the object. After a while Maired tried a a simple phrase, she took one of Lupinus' tunics and placed it on the floor. She asked Yrsa to pick it up. Yrsa smiled and did it, she looked so proud of herself for understanding.

Over the next few days, they spent any free time working on teaching Yrsa new words. Yrsa also spent time learning some of the tasks that needed to be done around the house. She surprised Maired with her ability to sew, she started with the mending but found some fabric and fashioned a small tunic for Lupinus.

"Ma sew," she said in a way of explanation. Maired took that to mean she was the daughter of a seamstress. Maired found it interesting that at such a young age Yrsa had learned to sew as well as she did.

"You're good," Maired said, Yrsa grinned and nodded. Over the next few days Maired took some of her extra money and bought fabric for Yrsa. She made small dresses and tunics. Maired sold them amongst the Christian community and gave Yrsa the profit.

"What use?" Yrsa said.

"Use for Yrsa," Maired said. She looked down at the few copper coins in

disbelief. "No tell Domine," Maired added
with a wink. Yrsa nodded solemnly.

Chapter 34
Litana

Moving day was a fun day! Litana had enjoyed a few nights in the roundhouse, it reminded her of when she was little. Today she was helping get things set up in the room in the caupona. She would share a room with the children, which made her happy. Litana loved the children, they didn't always know what was going on either.

Litana was organizing the linens and beds for the room. Llyr was helping her with moving the beds and deciding where they should go. Llyr was a good person too, she liked his brown hair that seemed to move like water on his head. He had a manly face too, and a friendly smile.

"Do you think you'll be ok against this wall?" Llyr asked as he placed a bed against the wall close to the entrance.

"I can be a guard," Litana said, making a mean face. Llyr laughed, she liked when he laughed, it was a kind laugh.

"The children are lucky to have you," Llyr said. Litana put some blankets on the bed Llyr had just put down. They were big wool blankets; she would be nice and warm. She could feel Llyr next to her, he was warm.

"I'm lucky to be here," Litana said. They had all treated her like she belonged. Taran and Samira had let her play with their boys and even let her take them on walks. She was always careful to stay on the road that always led to the caupona. She liked that it was hard to get lost.

Litana watched Llyr get the final bed into position and then remembered something she had wanted to say to him. When they were in the roundhouse, he had given her his bed and slept on the floor by the fire.

"Thank you for your bed," Litana said as Llyr stood up straight. He looked at her a little strangely and then smiled.

"It was no problem," Llyr said, "it was nice to have you stay with me." He stepped a little closer, he was standing right next to her. He was taller than her and she had to look up to see his eyes. She could also see up his nose, which made her giggle. Llyr angled his head so that she couldn't see up his nose. He was looking right down at her.

Litana could hear him breathing, she could smell him. He smelled like sweat and bread. She felt the heat coming from him again and looked up into his eyes. His eyes looked like two copper coins, shiny and brown. His lips looked like kisses. Litana wondered why she thought of kisses. Then she realized something.

"I think I want to kiss you," Litana said. She realized that a girl wasn't supposed to say something like that, but she wanted to.

"I'd like that," Llyr said softly. He leaned forwards and they kissed. Litana liked that his lips were a little firm but also soft. She wondered how he did that. She also liked that she felt warm and comfortable. She liked kissing him.

"What is going on here?" Maeli asked as she came into the room. Llyr jumped back as if he had been caught doing something wrong. Litana wondered if they shouldn't have kissed.

"Maeli," Llyr said, "I'm sorry, we were just." He stopped and looked at Litana and started a new sentence, "I wanted, or she wanted, I'm not sure what to say here." Litana did not understand that sentence at all.

"What were you doing?" Maeli asked. She sounded angry. Litana knew it was wrong.

"I'm sorry Domina," Litana said quickly, "I wanted to kiss him. He's so nice." Maeli seemed to calm down a little.

"I'm sorry Maeli," Llyr said, "she's so beautiful, I got a bit carried away." Litana couldn't believe what he said, he thought she was beautiful.

"I know she's beautiful," Maeli said, "but you can't take advantage of her." Litana wasn't sure what she meant.

"I wasn't trying to take advantage of her," Llyr said. They were getting loud, Litana didn't like them to fight.

"Maeli," Litana said, "please don't be mad."
Maeli was staring at Llyr and seemed to be ignoring her. Seren came into the room. Litana liked Seren, she was always smiling and laughing.

"What's wrong?" Seren asked frowning, "we can hear you from downstairs."

"I came up to find your son kissing Litana," Maeli said sternly. Seren turned to her son and got close to him.

"Is this true?" Seren asked.

"Ma," Llyr said, "I'm sorry, I don't think we did anything wrong. I like her and she likes me." He turned to Litana and asked, "you wanted to kiss me, didn't you?"

"She doesn't know what she wants!" Maeli said.

"Yes, I do!" Litana said. Maeli took her hand.

"Sweet child," Maeli said, "he is just using you. Like Domine Marcus"

"No, he didn't," Litana was close to tears, "I wanted him to kiss me."

"I don't think you know what you wanted," Maeli said gently. Litana couldn't believe Maeli would say this. She ran out of the room and down the stairs, she could feel the tears falling down her face but didn't care. She ran past everyone in the courtyard and into the bathhouse.

She slammed the door behind her and rushed down the corridor to the room where there were hot pipes on the wall spitting steam and a pool of very hot water. She sat on a bench, with the steam billowing all around her. She took off her cloak and threw it on the ground. It landed in the pool of hot water, but she didn't care.

She couldn't believe Maeli didn't think she wanted to kiss Llyr. She liked him, he was handsome, nice, funny and he didn't think she was stupid. Maeli thought she was stupid. Maeli was stupid!

Litana heard the door open and after a minute Maeli came into the room. She had taken the time to hang her cloak in the changing room. Maeli sat next to her for a moment and let out a long breath.

"Litana," Maeli said, "I'm sorry for what I said. I'm just worried that you might be hurt by him."

"Like Domine Marcus did?" Litana asked. She hadn't liked what Domine Marcus

had done to her. Every time he was alone
with her, he had touched her in places he
shouldn't. Either her chest or down below.
She knew it wasn't right but didn't want to get
into trouble. It had been trouble, like she
knew it would be. She had lost her best friend
and her favorite little boy.

"That's part of it," Maeli said. She was
looking at the cloak floating in the pool.
Litana hoped she wouldn't be mad about that
too. "I don't think Llyr is the same type of
man as Marcus," Litana agreed with that, Llyr
didn't even look at her the way Marcus had.

"I really did ask him to kiss me,"
Litana said. "I like him a lot." Maeli sighed
and turned to Litana.

"I'm just worried that he made you
think you wanted that," Maeli said. "Men can
do that sometimes. You must be careful."
Litana thought hard about that. She had to be
careful; she had to be smart.

"He thinks I'm funny," Litana said, "I
can make him laugh without doing something
dumb." Maeli's expression softened slightly.

"He's nice to you?" Maeli asked.

"Always," Litana said. She looked into
Maeli's eyes, hoping that Maeli would
understand. Her eyes got huge as she pleaded
quietly for her to understand.

"I think I need to talk to both of you together," Maeli said. She pointed at the cloak in the water, "we can fish that out later." Litana laughed softly. The ladies walked out to the courtyard where Llyr and Seren were sitting at a table. Maeli led Litana over and they joined them.

"Litana," Llyr said, "I apologize if I did anything that might hurt you. I don't want to hurt you at all. You are one of the sweetest, kindest people I know." Litana smiled at Llyr, her heart felt like it was exploding in her chest. She had never had anyone say such nice things to her.

"You didn't hurt me," Litana said, "I really like you too. I liked kissing you." There was a moment of complete silence, which made Litana feel a little uncomfortable. She didn't usually mind silence, but she wanted to know how much trouble she was in.

Maeli stood up and asked Seren to join her in the kitchen. She sat there uncomfortably with Llyr, not wanting to say anything. Teleri had been in the kitchen and Litana watched her run out of the caupona. She wished she knew what was going on.

Llyr sat staring at the table. Litana didn't like that she had gotten him into trouble, she should have just kept quiet. She wanted to go back to work in the room but didn't dare move. Soon Teleri came back with Owain. Litana did not realize she was in that much trouble.

Maeli came out from the kitchen and told Litana to head back up the stairs to keep working. Litana sighed in relief. She rushed up the stairs and started spreading blankets on all the beds. Teleri came up and joined her.

"What is going on?" Teleri asked quietly.

"I kissed Llyr," Litana said. Teleri made a face like she was sick and then smiled.

"You like him?" Teleri asked.

"Yes," Litana felt the heat in her cheeks. She was blushing.

"He likes you," Teleri said, "I can tell by the way he looks at you." Litana didn't know what to say to that and got to work organizing clothing and the few toys and games the children had.

She was almost done when she heard Maeli calling her. She slowly went down the stairs to find all the grownups sitting at the table, Llyr was standing close to them. He didn't look like he had been in trouble. Teleri quietly came down the stairs behind her.

"Litana," Maeli said, "we have something very important to ask you. You need to think about it and remember we will not be angry no matter what answer you

236

give." Litana was scared by this, she wasn't sure she could give the right answer. Maeli looked at Owain, who stood up and gently took her hand. She liked Owian, this couldn't be too bad.

"Litana," Owain said, "it's my duty as Llyr's father to find him a wife." Litana felt like her heart dropped in her chest. Had she made it so he couldn't marry? Was it because she let Domine Marcus touch her and she was dirty? "I'm wondering if you would be interested in becoming Llyr's wife." Litana wasn't sure what that meant. She was interested in becoming Llyr's wife. She liked him, was that a problem? She tried to think hard like Maeli said.

"I'm interested," Litana said slowly. "I'm not a good wife. I'm not smart."

"Neither is Llyr," Teleri said from where she was standing on the stairs.

"Teleri!" Seren scolded from her seat. Llyr seemed to understand what was going through Litana's head though. He walked over to Litana and stared into her eyes.

"Teleri's right," Llyr said, "sometimes I'm not smart. I do dumb things. I really like you though, which I think is smart." Teleri came down and put an arm around Litana's shoulder.

"If you like him too," Teleri said, "that would be smart. He's an annoying brother," Llyr shot her a look, "but he's a good man." Litana looked around at all the people waiting for her to talk.

"Can I marry you?" Litana finally asked Llyr.

"Of course you can," Llyr said, his smile spreading across his face.

"That's settled, I think," Owain said. He stood on the table and got everyone's attention. "Let the family know that Llyr is now betrothed to Litana." There was a cheer from the people moving things into the caupona. Litana wasn't sure what was going to happen next, but she knew she was going to be with Llyr.

Chapter 35
Yrsa

Marcus had been back for a day, and Yrsa could feel the tension in the insula. He was taking a break between assignments and had another two days before returning. Fortunately, he was spending most of his time taking Lupinus into town. Maired told Yrsa she was going to take her to the Christian community to meet some of the people there. Yrsa knew her Latin was now good enough for some polite conversation. She couldn't wait to try talking with other people.

The two walked through the city and down the alley to the building where Prisca kept a kitchen going to feed the members of the community. Yrsa was in awe of the big buildings they passed as they walked, she kept pointing at the columned buildings asking what they were.

Prisca greeted them loudly and brought them into her kitchen. When Yrsa greeted her in Latin, Prisca praised her use of the polite greeting. Yrsa felt so proud of herself. She also noticed that several of the children running around the large courtyard of the building were wearing tunics she had made. She now had a small purse of the

copper coins. She wasn't sure what she could
do with them, but she had them.

The ladies started to talk quickly and
Yrsa was soon lost. She had wondered what a
Christian was, Domina Maired had told her
that the word made Domine Marcus angry.
Yrsa didn't really know why, but she didn't
like talking to Domine Marcus, so she didn't
think she would use any words around him.

Marcus treated Yrsa like she was
stupid. She thought Marcus was stupid. He
had travelled all over the world and only
spoke one language. Lupinus, a child who
could barely talk, had already learned to speak
her language. She spoke the language of her
people and the language of the Angle people.
She was now learning the Roman language,
what they called Latin.

Yrsa noticed that the ladies were
looking at a stack of leather like the slavers
used. They were covered with strange runes.
Her father had tried to teach her to
understand the runes, but she had been very
small when he died. Her mother had lived a
little longer and taught her to sew and cook
before she died. Yrsa and her three brothers
tried to survive, but an uncle found them and
sold them all to the Romans. Yrsa asked what
the runes said.

"It's the story of our God," Maired explained. Yrsa wanted to know more but couldn't think of how to ask. Maired was explaining something, but Yrsa only understood that it was about a God who was bigger than other gods. She wondered if they meant Wodan, she knew that he was a powerful god. He travelled the world in disguise and took the dead from their rightful place.

When the time came to head home, Yrsa said a polite farewell to Prisca who told her that her Latin was getting very good. Yrsa followed Maired back down the streets. They were always so busy, people walking quickly. The smell was bad too, Yrsa didn't know why it smelled so bad, but there was always water in the street, standing water always had a bad smell, so that was probably the problem.

Maired stopped in front of one of the shops and looked behind at Yrsa. She turned and walked into the shop, Yrsa followed. It was a shop that sold fabric, Yrsa was very curious why they were here.

"Did you bring your coins?" Maired asked Yrsa.

"Yes," Yrsa said.

"Do you want to buy?" Maired pointed to the stacks of fabric, all folded neatly. There were so many colors and types

of fabric Yrsa felt like she had found a
treasure. Maired spoke to a man who took
them to the back where there was some linen
and wool fabric. They weren't colorful, just
plain, but Yrsa didn't care.

Yrsa felt all the fabric like she
remembered her mother doing. She knew she
was looking for imperfections and trying to
get a feel for how the fabric would fit. She
found a nice linen fabric that looked and felt
perfect. She knew she could make a pretty
dress with it. She pointed it out to the man.

He got it out and measured out some
of the fabric and said something Yrsa didn't
understand. Maired smiled and told Yrsa to
get her coins out. Maired helped her count
out some of the coins and handed them to the
man. He handed Yrsa the fabric.

Yrsa had understood they would be
trading for the fabric but didn't know why the
man wanted the coins. They were pretty but
didn't do anything. Yrsa remembered her Ma
trading clothes for food or clay pots, things
they could use. She couldn't imagine people
trading for those little coins. It didn't matter
though; she had her fabric.

Yrsa was in a good mood when they
got back to the insula. Lupinus was in his
room and got excited when Yrsa showed him
the fabric.

"What will you do with it," Lupinus asked.

"Make a dress," Yrsa said smiling. She got out the supplies she kept by her mat and started to look at the fabric. She liked planning out how best to cut the fabric so the dress would fall nicely. She took a break from her work to help Maired with some cleaning.

As she swept out the insula, Yrsa thought about the dress she would make. She could make it gather at her waist to make her look older. She had seen her mother do something similar and thought she could do it. If she had enough fabric left maybe she could drape some to look like the Roman palla, the long wrap women wore.

Yrsa couldn't get back to sewing until Lupinus was asleep. She lit a lantern and used the dim light to help her sew. She knew she should sleep, but she was excited and didn't feel tired. Lupinus kept stirring in his bed, Yrsa was afraid the light would bother him.

Yrsa decided to take the lamp and her sewing to the cenaculum. She wasn't really supposed to be there during the night, but everyone was asleep. She snuck out, being careful not to make any noise. Setting up in the cenaculum was easy and Yrsa got back to sewing. She was moving quickly and had the main part of the dress stitched and wanted to try it on to make sure it would fit and figure out how to gather it. She knew she should go back into the cubiculum to try it on, but Lupinus was asleep in there. She didn't want to risk waking him. She took off her dress and picked up the new dress. She heard a noise behind her.

Domine Marcus was standing in the doorway of his cubiculum staring at her. Yrsa dropped the dress and tried to cover up with her arms. Marcus said something she didn't understand and took a step towards her, Yrsa knew she was in trouble. He picked up the new dress and looked at it, she thought about grabbing for it, but knew that would cause more trouble.

"I'm sorry," Yrsa said softly. Domine Marcus smiled and nodded. Maybe it was fine that she was working out here. Marcus sat down on a reclinium, still holding the dress. He held it up in front of her, did he want to see what it would look like on her? He was saying something, Yrsa tried to understand.

"Try it," was what she finally understood. He was still holding it so Yrsa didn't know how to try it on.

Domine Marcus just sat there staring at her. He didn't hand her the new dress to try on, she reached for it but it was out of reach. He said something else she didn't understand

and had an evil grin on his face. He was
pulling on his own tunic; Yrsa could see his
thigh in the lamplight when suddenly the
world seemed to explode with noise.

Maired was standing behind Domine
Marcus, she was shouting something. Marcus
stood and dropped the dress; Yrsa picked it
up and tried to get it on. In her rush she tore a
seam in the new dress. She ran into her
cubiculum as the shouting continued. She was
petrified and curled up into a ball on her mat.

The yelling continued until finally she
heard the front door slam. Maired came in
and sat next to her rubbing her back. Yrsa
cried, she had no idea what she had done
wrong, but it must have been terrible.

Chapter 36
Maired

Maired stormed around the room, she was angrier than she had ever been in her life. When she had come in and found her husband with the girl, she felt as if her heart had stopped. He claimed that she had been in the room with no clothes on and he was trying to help her get dressed. She didn't believe it!

The argument had been brief as Maired was not going to accept any excuse that he had. She told him she was not going to let him abuse another slave. She would send her away. He told her she couldn't because Yrsa was his slave and not hers. She claimed he had told her it was a gift and she could do what she wanted. He had told her that she was his woman and could only do what he said she could do. Maired had almost hit him when he said that. He stormed out of the insula before she could hit him.

Now she was starting to calm down and was trying to breathe normally again. She took deep breaths, still pacing across the floor. She had heard about Roman men buying slaves for the purpose of such pleasures, but thought Marcus was better than that. She couldn't trust him and would find a way to send Yrsa away. She had to, she loved that child. She just had to calm down enough to think it through.

The door to Yrsa and Lupinus' cubiculum opened and the girl walked in. Her face showed that she had been crying for some time.

"Sorry Domina," Yrsa said, "please, I'm sorry." Maired sat down and beckoned the girl over.

"My child," Maired said, "you don't need to be sorry."

"I was wrong," Yrsa said, "I stayed up after sleep time. I wanted dress." She had taken off her new dress and put on her slaves tunic before coming out. She felt that she was not worth having her own dress.

"You shouldn't have stayed up," Maired said, "but Domine Marcus was also wrong. He should not have touched you."

"I was scared," Yrsa said quietly. "Maybe I am wrong." Maired shook her head.

"You weren't wrong," Maired said, "it was scary." Yrsa fell into Maired's arms and the two sat together for a while embracing. Maired calmed down a little; she could feel that Yrsa was falling asleep in her arms. Maired lay down on the reclinium and she nodded off too.

She woke as Marcus came back into the cenaculum. He glared at her as he walked past her and into their cubiculum. No apologies, no admission of guilt, just a door in the face. Maired shifted Yrsa so she could get up. She walked into her room to find Marcus lying in the bed.

"I can't have you hurting girls in my home," Maired said sternly. "You need to stop or I will stop you." Marcus sat up and glared at her, as if daring her to do something.

"What are you going to do?" Marcus asked. "You are a nobody. You trapped me into this marriage. Most legionaries are out there meeting women and having fun. I'm here with you."

"I gave you a son!" Maired said. "You like him, don't you?"

"Lupinus isn't a part of this," Marcus said, "your brother used him to force me to marry you. I could have had a dozen sons with a dozen women!"

"Seems like that is what you are trying to do," Maired spat.

"What do you want me to say?" Marcus said, "that you are so beautiful that I am happy here."

"So, leave," Maired said. She wasn't sure why she said it, but it came out. She did want him to leave, but what would happen to

her if he did. If he divorced her, he could take
Lupinus. Maired was afraid of losing
everything she had, but she did not want to
spend another moment with this man.

"I will!" Marcus said. "Goodnight!"
turned and walked out of the insula. The
conversation was over. Maired wasn't sure if
she should follow him or just let him calm
down.

Maired went to Lupinus' cubiculum
and got into bed with him. She looked down
at his unruly hair; it was the same color as hers
and she realized she might never see him
again. She wept quietly until she couldn't stay
awake any longer.

The next morning Maired woke to
find Marcus gone. Yrsa was in the cenaculum
setting out some bread and cheese. She smiled
at Maired as if nothing had happened.
Lupinus was helping her. Her world was
seemingly unchanged. The door to the insula
slowly opened and Marcus came in. Maired
braced herself to hear he was taking her son
and leaving. He beckoned her to follow him
into their cubiculum. She followed meekly
behind him. When the door closed, she saw
that Marcus looked tired, but she couldn't
read his emotions at all.

"Maired," Marcus said softly, "I did
not sleep at all. After I left, I went out for a

long walk." Marcus sat on the bed and put his head in his hands. Maired stood by the door and waited, not willing to accept one part of his little sob story.

"I'm sorry to hear that," Maired said coldly.

"You were right," Marcus said, "I let myself get carried away when I saw her in my home undressed."

"That is no excuse," Maired said softly.

"Maybe you're right," Marcus said looking up at Maired, she could see he had been crying, he was now. She could not believe he was so manipulative, to cry in front of her. "I shouldn't have done what I did."

"You're right," Maired said sternly.

"I am leaving," Marcus said, "for a while. I'm moving to the barracks today. I spend most of my time there anyway."

"Fine," Maired said before turning and going through the door. She was not about to allow herself to be manipulated by that monster. She told Yrsa and Lupinus they were going out. They walked to a bakery that sold some of Lupinus' favorite sweet breads and sat there to eat. Lupinus told Maired about his dream the night before, and Maired smiled. She asked him about what he thought they should do for the rest of the day. He suggested the Circus Maximus; it was what he always wanted to do and was surprised when his mother agreed. They rushed to the insula to get dressed, Marcus had already left, to Maired's relief. Maired gave Yrsa a small dress to wear.

"Today we are going to pretend you are my daughter," Maired said. "Won't that be a fun game?" Lupinus clapped.

"Sister Yrsa!" Lupinus said laughing. The dress was a little big, so they quickly pinned it up and rushed to the circus. The crowds were lined up to enter the big building when they arrived and Lupinus could barely contain his excitement. He was a fan of the famous charioteer Scorpus, who was racing today.

Their seats were high up, and they could see the entire track. The only way to tell the difference between chariots was the color of the chariot and the feathers on the horses. Maired listened to Lupinus explain to Yrsa that Scorpus wore red and they were cheering for him. The chariots lined up and the crowd became deafening. Lupinus was standing on his seat yelling. A horn sounded and the race began. The red team took an early lead. Maired never understood the appeal of chariot races, but Yrsa's reaction amused her.

Yrsa joined in Lupinus' excitement and cheered as the red team lapped the white team. She didn't really understand it all but was caught up in the excitement. The stress of the night before melted as she allowed herself to become part of the crowd and cheered on Scorpus. There were three races that day, and Lupinus was overjoyed that he was allowed to stay for all three. Yrsa kept looking at Maired as if in awe that after all that went on, they were having fun today. She didn't know the inner turmoil that Maired was experiencing. After the first race, Maired just sat and wondered what would have been different if she had told Marcus that she found him annoying and to leave her alone.

She would be at the caupona now. Likely married to a boy from the area. She would not have Lupinus, the great chariot race enthusiast and champion knucklebone player. She would not have met Litana, wherever she was. She would not have met Yrsa. Life was hard, but she would survive.

Chapter 37
Llyr

Llyr woke to the sound of the door to the old slave quarters opening. He looked over to see Litana struggling to carry a tray through the door. The door swung shut on her and knocked the tray onto the floor, ale, bread and cheese went everywhere. Litana looked upset and got down quickly to clean it up. Llyr came to help her, she was starting to cry.

"I wanted to bring my husband some food," Litana said. "It's my job as your wife." Llyr felt sorry that she hadn't succeeded, he could tell she had tried.

"You are the best wife ever!" Llyr said, putting an arm around Litana. "Thank you for bringing me food."

"It's all on the floor," Litana said, pointing at the mess.

"It is," Llyr said nodding. "Just how I like it." Llyr grabbed the bread off the floor and tore the loaf open before going to take a bite.

"That is disgusting," Litana said with a laugh. Llyr smiled and kissed Litana. He helped her clean up. They would need to move out as soon as he had built a roundhouse, but for now the old slave

quarters was their home. After the mess was
cleaned up Llyr started to get dressed.

The courtyard was busy as everyone
was preparing to open the caupona. The past
week they had focused on the wedding, but
Taran had insisted that they open for guests.
Llyr found Taran and the two went to the
stable together to finish the project he had
been helping with. Ceredig and the carpenter,
Tegid, had built a sign for the caupona. Llyr
had worked with them to make certain that
the triskelion was carved correctly and the
name was placed on it properly.

They carried the sign out of the arch,
where a bar was placed on the wall. The bar
jutted out towards the street, when the sign
was hanging off it, they would be able to see it
walking towards the inn from either side. Llyr
climbed a ladder that was against the wall and
helped Taran to hang the sign.

There were people from the
community standing out front of the caupona
who cheered as the sign went up. The
Caupona Caureni was once more open.
People piled through the arch to see the new
building.

The day was filled with hard work and
laughter as people ate Samira's exotic cooking
and listened to Taran's stories. Llyr kept a
close eye on Litana who was serving drinks to

the customers. She was also a natural in dealing with people, making them feel at ease. Llyr was not a people person and stayed back to care for any animals that might come in.

Llyr had never really been a part of the running of the caupona, and would one day take over his father's dairy. Today was special for him, to see his family coming together to keep this part of their family alive. Litana obviously enjoyed being a part of the caupona as well. He would make sure she was able to continue until they had children.

Like any good day, the time went quickly and before they knew it, they had two guests staying the night and everyone else was gone. Maeli and Seren sat at the table in the kitchen looking tired but content. Taran was in the tabiculum, a little room off the kitchen where they counted the earnings. Sabrina and Riva came down the stairs; the children all tucked in their beds. Teleri and Ceredig were building a fire for any guests that wanted to sit in the courtyard.

Litana found Llyr in the stable, feeding the only horse brought by a guest. She watched him work for a while before walking over to him and smiling.

"Your mother has asked you to join her," Litana said.

"Your mother as well," Llyr said, taking her hand and leading her to the kitchen. Everyone slowly took a seat around the table. Seren stood and looked around at the crowd.

"When my father came here," Seren said, "he was given a part ownership of this caupona as a reward. Maeli was given the other part ownership when her friend passed away. This caupona has become a part of this family. I pray that it will remain so for many years to come." Everyone voiced their agreement. Llyr looked at Litana, his family now. He wondered what the future would bring for this old inn.

Coming Soon from D.W. Lewis

Home

Book IV of the Caerwyn Chronicles

Coming September of 2026

The following is a preview of Home

Nura picked up another long linen cloth off the floor. She did not understand how men could be so messy, technically her brother Malik was supposed to have all this cleaned up. The lady's hour for the bathhouse started soon and he had left quickly after spending the day helping the men. Bathhouse attendant was one of the easiest jobs in their families caupona and also one of the worst.

There were only a few women in the community that used the bathhouse, most of them older. They would be waiting for the time scheduled for them, lined up at the door. Nura had spent all day in the kitchen and now had a few more hours in here until her work was done. If she had enough energy she might meet up with her friends after she was done.

The ladies came in and Nura helped those that struggled with changing into the linen togas they offered for modesty. Nura was glad all the women used them, Malik complained that some men did not. She helped the ladies pick out scented oils for their skin, keeping a mental record of what they were using. Her father had taught her to make sure they have a good record of what people use so they can charge the right amount. The frankincense oils cost more than the rose oils, so they made sure people that used it were charged extra.

The door to the bathhouse opened and Nura rushed to the changing room to see if

anyone would need help. She was a little
surprised to see Elen, her friend.

"What are you doing here?" Nura asked.

"I came to make sure you joined us
today," Elen said. "A group of us are going to
the river." It was a hot day, and even hotter in
the bathhouse, a trip to the river would be
welcome. Nura was thankful that the sun stayed
up longer on warm days.

"I will join you there," Nura said, "as
soon as I clean up here."

"See you there!" Elen said before
ducking back out the door. Nura returned to her
duties keeping the bathhouse customers happy.
Most of them were in the hot pool now, so her
job was keeping clean and getting cool water or
ale for those that got thirsty.

The ladies often used this time to share
news from the community. Nura would sit and
listen as they discussed betrothals and new
children being born. They also discussed the
scandals, they enjoyed those the most. Nura
laughed quietly at the ladies, this evening at the
river she would be having similar conversations
with her friends. Age didn't change people as
much as her mother implied.

With the extreme heat outside, the ladies
did not linger in the hot pool and moved quickly
into the corridor to head to the cold plunge bath.
Nura helped some of the ladies make their way
to the cold plunge, relieved that the time spent in
here was almost over.

As the last of the ladies dressed, Nura hurriedly cleaned up and rushed to the tabiculum. The tabiculum was a small room off the kitchen that stood across the courtyard of the caupona. Her father, Taran, sat there waiting for her, his grey hair and beard shining in the lamplight. This room had no windows for security; it was the room where the money was stored.

Nura gave her father a rundown of which lady had used which oils, and he wrote them down on a wax tablet. The tablet was a big piece of wax in a wooden frame; he could record figures on it and then when he was ready for a new day he melt the wax and started over. He smiled, his brown eyes glistening.

"Well done, Nura," Taran said.

"Thank you Da," Nura replied, "can I head to the river with some friends?"

"Yes," Taran said, "have fun." Nura kissed her father on the forehead. It used to feel strange to her that she was taller than he was, she stood taller than most men. Her brothers would tease her about broad shoulders and square jaw, saying she looked like a man. The boys in town seemed intimidated by her size as well, but her darker skin that she got from her Nabatean mother and copper colored hair still made her feel beautiful.

Nura ran to the room she shared with her grandmother to change from a work dress to a simple wool dress that had a frayed hem. She wanted something that would not be ruined by the mud. As she rushed out her brother, Ramon, asked where she was going in a hurry, but she just waved him off. The last thing she needed was him trying to come with her; this trip to the river was girls only!

The river was a short walk through the heavily wooded area behind the caupona. Nura loved the quiet forest trail, there were no guests demanding ale, no brothers annoying her and no parents to tell her what to do next. Just her and nature. She could hear the girls before she saw them, they were enjoying wading and swimming in the river.

"You made it," Elen called as Nura walked up to the riverbank.

"The bathhouse was too hot today," Nura said, "the old ladies didn't want to stay." Elen laughed and came out of the water. Nura removed her wool dress, leaving on her linen under tunic. It came to her knees and would be modest enough in the water. Still, she was glad there were no boys around.

There were four other girls splashing and wading in the water, cooling off after long days working in their homes. Elen was one of the girls in the group who was most liked, her long brown hair and blue eyes, with her short nose and round face made her beautiful but not so beautiful that she wasn't likable.

"Any good gossip from the bathhouse?" Elen asked.

"Not really," Nura said as they eased into the cold water. "They all wanted to talk about Ramon and Coria's betrothal." Elen laughed and splashed Coria, who was lying in the water nearby.

"Hear that, Coria?" Elen asked.

"Who cares," Coria said. She stood up, the water dripping off her golden braids. Ramon had told Nura that her golden hair and green eyes were the most beautiful he had seen. She was sixteen and had blemished skin and a line of freckles across her straight nose. Nura liked her and was happy she was betrothed to her brother.

"Exactly," Nura said. She lay down and floated down the river on her back. She stared up at the clouds floating by. She was a little upset that Ramon was betrothed before she was. Her father had tried, but most men found her size to be intimidating. She let herself relax and think about other things.

She thought about her cousin Artor, who had left home to travel a few years back. They had been so close over the years, but he had no interest in settling down and having a family in Caerwyn. She wondered what he was doing now. She wondered if he had the right idea about not marrying and exploring the world.

Since no men seemed interested, Nura wondered if she should find a way to explore the world. It wasn't as easy for a woman, but her mother had always shown her that a woman was just as capable as a man. Nura could see herself traveling to Petra, where she had lived as a small child and exploring the desert with her mother's family.

The sun was setting, and Nura realized that the other girls had already left. She stood up and walked back to where her dress was neatly folded on a bush. As she reached for it she sensed some movement in the trees just beyond the shoreline. She wondered if it was a deer and moved quietly to see what it was. She could just see a shadow moving back into the trees. Whatever it was, it was big.

It was also moving away so Nura decided it wasn't a threat. Nura slipped her dress over her wet under tunic, which was uncomfortable, but the sun was setting and she didn't have time to dry off. She started walking into the woods when she heard another sound. She stopped and tried to see what was out there. There was something in the shadows, she could just see it.

Nura slowed down, not sure what was in the forest. The shadows were getting longer, and she couldn't see as well in the dark forest. She got down low and squinted ahead to see if there was something she should be aware of. Her hand went to where she normally kept a knife on her belt, but in her rush to come out she had forgotten it. She was out there without a way to defend herself.

Nura was mad at herself for getting into this situation. She thought back to the idea of exploring the world on her own. She would have to become better at preparing for danger. A twig snapped and Nura jumped, she could see a person now. He was smaller than she was, maybe she could fight him.

The leaves rustled and Malik jumped out at her. Nura screamed and punched him in the jaw.

"Ow!" Malik shouted, rubbing his jaw. His jaw was becoming more masculine as he was maturing. With his dark complexion and dark curls, Nura knew several girls that were hoping he would notice them.

"Serves you right for scaring me," Nura said. She was still shaking, but the look on her brother's face made her chuckle.

"I was sent to escort you home," Malik said, still rubbing his jaw. "Da thinks you need protection." He laughed in spite of himself, he had argued his sister was not the type that needed protection, but his father had insisted he go. He was happy to know that he was right.

"Why did you startle me," Nura said.

"I thought it would be funny," Malik said laughing. Nura lightly punched his shoulder again and the two walked back towards home.

If you are enjoying the Caerwyn Chronicles:
learn more at www.caerwynchronicles.com